KATHRYN SCANLAN

THE DOMINANT ANIMAL

Kathryn Scanlan is the author of *Aug 9—Fog*. Her work has been published in *NOON*, *Fence*, *Granta*, *The Iowa Review*, and *The Paris Review*. She lives in Los Angeles.

ALSO BY KATHRYN SCANLAN

Aug 9—Fog

THE

DOMINANT

ANIMAL

THE

DOMINANT

ANIMAL

Stories

KATHRYN SCANLAN

MCD X FSG ORIGINALS

FARRAR, STRAUS AND GIROUX

NEW YORK

MCD × FSG Originals
Farrar, Straus and Giroux
120 Broadway, New York 10271

Library of Congress Cataloging-in-Publication Data
Names: Scanlan, Kathryn, 1980– author.
Title: The dominant animal : stories / Kathryn Scanlan.
Description: New York, New York : MCD × FSG Originals /
    Farrar, Straus and Giroux, [2020]
Identifiers: LCCN 2019054462 | ISBN 9780374538293 (paperback)
Subjects: LCSH: Flash fiction, American. | Short stories, American.
Classification: LCC PS3619.C263 .A6 2020 | DDC 813/.6—dc23
LC record available at https://lccn.loc.gov/2019054462

Designed by Gretchen Achilles

Our books may be purchased in bulk for promotional, educational,
or business use. Please contact your local bookseller or the Macmillan
Corporate and Premium Sales Department at 1-800-221-7945, extension 5442,
or by e-mail at MacmillanSpecialMarkets@macmillan.com.

www.fsgoriginals.com • www.fsgbooks.com
Follow us on Twitter, Facebook, and Instagram at @fsgoriginals

1   3   5   7   9   10   8   6   4   2

To Ruby

CONTENTS

THE FIRST WHIFFS OF SPRING   3

THE CANDIDATE   6

BEEF HEARTS TRIMMED OF FAT, BRAISED   11

PLAYHOUSE   15

HAPPY WIFE, HAPPY LIFE   18

◆

FLORIDA IS FOR LOVERS   21

MEN OF THE WOODS   25

SMALL PINK FEMALE   30

POWER TOOLS   32

SHH   34

◆

MOTHER'S TEETH   39

THE BABY   44

PLEASE 46

BAIT-AND-SWITCH 49

THE IMPRECATION 52

◆

DEAR SIRS 57

COLONIAL REVIVAL 60

THE LOCKET 63

THE HUNGRY VALLEY 65

VICTORIAN WEDDING PORTRAIT 68

◆

BJ 73

COOLLY, BLUELY 76

LINE 80

DERLAND 82

THE DOMINANT ANIMAL 85

◆

SALAD DAYS 93

LIVE A LITTLE 97

DESIGN FOR A CARPET 101

THE WINE MANAGER AND I 103

TA-DA! 104

◆

YET YOU TURN TO THE MAN 109

VAGRANTS 111

NOW THIS 114

DEAR MARY 115

THE OLD MILL 117

◆

FABLE 123

MASTER FRAMER 128

THE RESCUED MAN 131

LEMONS 135

THE POKER 137

ACKNOWLEDGMENTS 145

THE

DOMINANT

ANIMAL

THE FIRST WHIFFS OF SPRING

I took a bus past the old dairy with the big metal cow out front. The cow had long, thick eyelashes and pink-painted lips like a human woman's. On the cow's head was a pillowy, blue-spotted bonnet topped with a large, floppy bow.

Hey, I called to the bus driver. Everyone else had gotten off earlier, at the hospital.

Hey, I said. Why do you think they want that cow to look like a human woman? No ideas? I said.

You can't be drinking that in here, he said without looking up.

I pinched my own lips in a pucker and sucked air into my mouth. Then I let out the long, suggestive whistle I'd recently learned.

Where I was going—it was something to do with a family. It may have been my family. When I arrived, there was a

3

large frosted cake, boxes of wine, and a pyramid of sparkling plastic flutes.

I swallowed some flutes of wine and from a metal platter lifted a single cube of orange cheese that someone had taken the time to stab with a little pick.

I walked the perimeter of the room and leaned on a wall beneath a large, unrecognizable flag. On the dance floor, several people were creeping around in the dark. A hectic pattern of lighted dots fell all over them.

In the bathroom, someone had painted bright, childish flowers along the bottom of the wall, giving the impression that the flowers were growing from the linoleum floor. The hand soap had left a bright pink puddle on the sink. Its cherry smell made me wish for something pink to drink. It mingled with a septic odor that emanated from the old lidless toilets.

I was wearing a dress, a purse, shoes. Earrings. Some bracelets. A large, elaborate brooch. Barrettes and clips. Rings. A belt upon which I'd set my hopes of pulling everything together.

People sang. Several individuals, working together, lit a large quantity of candles.

Then, the swaddled body landed in my arms—somebody's new, red baby—another stranger brought into the world. Here was the cause of our celebration.

I looked down at its swollen face, its unseeing eyes. It waved an arm stiffly.

Smells of mud and manure were coming through the open

windows—the first whiffs of spring. When I went outside, the wind began to blow. It was coming from a long way off with nothing to stop it. It turned me around. It opened my mouth. It undid my hair and lifted my skirt. It scattered me just like I liked.

THE CANDIDATE

The father was a professional manipulator of spinal bones and the mother was a skilled scraper, dauber, and suctionist. They enjoyed playing together: tennis and golf, as well as games of chance. They were slim and tan and drove sporty European cars. One didn't mind his lack of hair, because he had physical vigor and a nicely shaped head—or maybe it was his money. She kept her hair chemically kinky—a nonchalant frizz.

In the morning they liquefied fruits and in the evening they steamed leaves and heads in a large metal pot. The breast of a bird—split, skinned—turned slowly in the dim yellow theater of the microwave oven.

There was a dog, of course. It was big and blond with an expensive heritage. The dog's name—it eludes me, but it was something to do with victory, royalty, luxury.

And there were two children—an adolescent boy and a prepubescent girl.

I was blond, too, but of a different sort. My pedigree was mixed. For a brief period, they tried me. They took me on a trip with them—all of us together in a large van with a small television in the back. A second adolescent boy was auditioning as well.

We drove for a day, then arrived at the stucco condo that was to be the site of our happiness and relaxation.

I understood my role as companion to the girl, but my exuberances could not excite her. She watched me with the disinterest of the statistician she would become.

To the mother and father I went then, but because they had recently cleaned themselves and put on fresh, light-colored clothing, my approach caused a great deal of alarm.

The boys, then, I could not avoid. At the pool, they bared their hideous bodies to swim or just because it was hot and they were proud. They strutted—huge and spindly, jackal-faced, inflamed, malformed. They called to me.

I dropped straight in. When I tried to come up, they held me down as long as was funny. I understood this as their birthright. On they would go—a lifetime of dunking, of the pleasures of the dunker.

I suppose I was asking for it—the way I would hide beneath a piece of furniture and cry out when frightened. I was easily riled. It didn't take much to spook me. I was a soft thing, very grabbable, with large, wet eyes and a tender nose. At mealtime, I ate at top speed, jealously eyeing the bowls and plates and the rates at which they emptied into mouths other than my own. Here was a group of individuals who took their time with food and did not appear to derive any particular enjoyment from consuming it. In a corner, the dog daintily took its kibble, coin by coin, and never approached the table to beg.

The day we were to go out on the motorboat, the girl began to bleed. The mother took her into a rest-stop bathroom and stood outside the stall while the girl attempted to insert what her mother had given her. The girl cried. She said she could not do it. This went on.

The phenomenon had recently been explained to us in the music room at school, where many of the female teachers, as well as most of the mothers, had assembled one afternoon. On a table at the front of the room sat a large human torso—gruesomely separated from the rest of its body—vivisected to reveal the organs, which were brightly colored and removable.

The lights were dimmed and a movie was projected onto a screen. In the movie, some girls had a sleepover at a friend's house. The friend's mother poured pancake batter into a hot frying pan in the morning. She made a large pancake in the shape of the female reproductive system to illustrate what had happened to one of the girls in the night. Then, together, they ate the pancakes.

The lights were turned on again. Blood, sanitary napkins, and the importance of personal hygiene were discussed.

Otherwise, I said loudly, you might start attracting flies.

The teachers and mothers—my mother—all turned to look at me then. It was a look I have come to recognize.

My companion emerged at last—triumphant but shaken. Mother and daughter washed their hands in happy communion, talking to each other's reflection in the mirror. Then they turned and saw that I was still leaning on the wall, cramped between two dryers. There came a change in posture like a sigh.

Come along, clipped the mother. The boys have waited long enough.

We were late getting out on the water. It was crowded with other boats and ours burned your arm if you leaned on it. The father popped a beer and revved the motor. We bounced along.

At last the father found us some solitude. One by one, they dove gracefully into the water and surfaced laughing. They floated and flipped their bodies around. The father did it one-handed, his beer held aloft.

I stood at the edge of the boat. The steps dissolved into thick green water. I wore a man's heavy T-shirt over my bathing suit. I said it was because I burned quickly, which was also true.

Come on! shouted the father.

Do it! shouted his boy.

Little baby! shouted the second boy.

The dog barked and drank the water in huge gulps.

The girl and her mother swam quietly around each other. The girl disappeared first. When they emerged, they were far away—a pair of slicked, shining heads moving quickly out of the picture.

Now the mother is dead. The dog is dead. The girl has a little boy. The boy has two wives and three girls. The father has a new dog and a new wife and a new house. The second boy has all of these—and more. Like so many things in my head, this information arrived uninvited, and insists on hanging around.

BEEF HEARTS TRIMMED OF FAT,
BRAISED

Do we have anything to eat? he asked.

There's some cornflakes, I said. In the cupboard.

He got the box of cornflakes and poured some into a bowl. He poured a little milk onto them. He stood holding the bowl with one hand, and with the other, he got a spoon. He dug in.

These are terrible, he shouted.

I can't hear you, I said.

They're completely stale, he said. Ugh, they're really bad.

He finished the flakes in the bowl, then finished the flakes in the box and flattened the box and rinsed the bowl and set it by the sink.

Later he said, I'm still hungry. Why don't we have anything to eat in this house?

There's plenty to eat, I said.

Like what, for example? he said.

Just look, I said. Just look around.

Then I heard him opening and closing doors and drawers. There was the light suctioning sound of the refrigerator and freezer.

After a while, he came to where I was, holding a foil-wrapped bar to his mouth. He gripped the unwrapped end between his teeth and grimaced. The bar—brown, dense, lightly flecked—would not give way.

He tossed it into the small waste bin in the corner, where it made a loud sound when it struck.

Where did you even find that? I asked.

You hid it from me, he said, a long time ago, and then you forgot about it. That's what I think.

Why would I do that? I said. But I often hid things from him, because if I didn't, he would eat everything all at once, in a single day—in one sitting, even.

At that moment, for example, I had a sack of cashews in my underwear drawer, an unopened bag of pretzel rods in an empty shoebox at the back of the bedroom closet, three chocolate bars folded into the kitchen towels in the pantry, and a large, costly wedge of aged cheese wrapped in cloth in an unused corner of the unheated basement, where I crept with a knife when he was in the bathroom or occupied by the television.

When we dined out, we dined exclusively at all-you-can-eat establishments. You got your table—then, without even sitting down, you approached the food arrayed beneath the hot flood of gold light. Here were spiny creatures carted up from the bottom of the ocean. Here were the most succulent

sections of a whole herd of ungulates and run-of-the-mill vegetables and fruits prepared in ways you'd never trouble with
at home. You made your selection, and it gave you a sense of
yourself. No one's plate looked like yours.

I ate quickly. In the end, however, I never ate much. I
would finish in a matter of minutes, but he ate much more
slowly, chewing thoughtfully, a distance runner.

Are you done, really? he would ask.

Yes, I would say. I'm very full.

I would sit drinking ice water while he went back for a
second, third, fourth, and sometimes fifth plate of food.

He sat in a relaxed posture—unhurried, one hand flat
upon the table while the other rose and fell. I suppose he cost
the establishment a good deal of money.

In fact, not long after we became regulars at one particular restaurant, the price of the buffet increased from $12.95
to $15.95, so we stopped going there.

It was a pity, because it was my favorite. There was a very
grand feeling it gave you. On each table was a little lamp in
the shape of a dripping wax candle. At the top of the lamp
was a clear glass bulb like a flame, with an orange filament
flickering inside, and at the base was a small button that,
when pressed, summoned a busboy to your table lickety-split.

On our last visit there, after four glasses of water, I made a
trip to the bathroom. I glided along—past the other diners—
admiring the patterned carpet, the gilded wallpaper, and the
glossy plastic plants, the leaves of which looked to have been
regularly wiped of dust.

Daylight came through the front wall of windows, which went all the way up to the ceiling. The windows were framed by the tallest drapes I'd ever seen, heavy velvet brocade, held in place by gold-tasseled ropes.

The blinds on the windows were discreetly raised or lowered by the busboys depending on the angle of the sun. Two of the boys were working to lower them, tenderly tugging the cords and releasing the slack.

Just past the busboys, I saw him. He was chewing—then he stopped. He seemed to be darkening—dwindling. He squinted, then turned his face up and sniffed.

We drove home with the defroster blasting. In my mouth, with my tongue, I found something small and sharp—stubbornly planted—up in a place I couldn't reach.

PLAYHOUSE

They are a family of four, our neighbors, with one biological son and one adopted, but so near in age and similar in appearance it seems a little funny, as if the parents had their minds set on twins. The boys do not like each other and they do not like their parents and their parents do not like each other and they do not like their sons, neither one of them.

In the morning as the father backs his car into the street, one son runs from the house and throws himself onto the hood. The father honks until the boy rolls off, sullen, his arms hanging like clubs. Inside the house the mother will scream for minutes at a go. We have our hands on the phone to call someone about it. But then she stops, steps out onto the patio, sits and props her feet onto the ottoman, and lights a cigarette. Her hair is smooth and her clothes look pressed and cool.

Sometimes comes the surprise of another day, another night ending, quietly, and without incident. The father returns from work and drinks a beer on the patio. The boys play basketball in the drive. The mother flips pieces of food on the grill. But in the small hours of the morning, one son is chasing the other in the yard with a pair of scissors. It is early enough that we could be dreaming it, the half-clad boys running and tumbling like satyrs in the blue light of the lawn. Our dream disperses when the father bangs out of the house, puffed up, trailing his untied bathrobe. He throws his arms around the scissor carrier, and they topple into the grass together.

At any hour, the father can be seen tending his property. We've awakened at midnight to the sound of his mower. There is little in the way of ornament, though the shrubs are kept neatly cubed.

Between their lawn and ours is a child's playhouse, sturdily built, with real glass windows and a slide and two swings. When the snow melts in bleak spring, the father sands the sides of the family's house and the playhouse and touches up the peeled places. He stands on a ladder, using the same paint, a medium milky brown, for both buildings.

In the early evening when daylight lingers a little longer than it did the day before, when the father has finished his work and put away his tools and stands in his bare brown yard, appraising, we see how the two structures look like two of the same animal, large and small, grown and juvenile, or parent and offspring.

On an afternoon while the parents are away, the boys are outside doing things they are forbidden to do. Slowly they start to shove each other toward the playhouse. They stand in front of it a while, throwing pieces of grass as hard as they're able, but the grass only falls peacefully to their feet. They sit on the swing seats, their bottoms hanging out the backs and their ankles dragging under them.

The boys stand and put their hands on the playhouse. They grab it and mount their long bodies onto it, rocking it from its rutted resting place. They climb inside. We can see wedges of them pressed up to the glass. The playhouse shudders on its stilted legs, and the boys do not come out. The sun drops into the trees and the grass goes dark.

When the parents return, the car's beams swing across the lawns—ours and theirs—and come to rest at the raw, un-fenced spot where the playhouse sits. The mother and father wait with the engine running. The ungainly thing begins to tremble, then one boy drops out and stumbles into our early flesh-pink rhododendron. The other son follows and falls face-first into our bleeding heart. There is some permanent damage.

Our house is similar in color to our neighbor's—awkward and glass-fronted. The houses on our block are not old but look vaguely historical, all built, it seems, with no concern other than getting the best possible view of the sunset.

HAPPY WIFE, HAPPY LIFE

When my wife died I did not want to live, so when my heart stopped I thought, Good. But my daughter took me to the hospital and they opened my chest and found me in there.

My wife would say, Arguing with you is like talking to a bowl of potatoes! So I would argue with her sometimes just to make her happy.

FLORIDA IS FOR LOVERS

My parents wanted me out from the start. In good weather they turned me loose at dawn to wander door to door. I was liked by neighbor women with grown children—they'd put me on their laps and feed me sticky rolls and milky coffee while they smoked and talked about their husbands. At dusk—with reluctance—my parents unbolted their home and whistled for me to come. They kept me in the basement in a large room with a tiled floor and a window that looked onto the ground of the backyard, where I watched their sandaled feet cross and uncross in the grass.

When they rid themselves of me at last—when I stood with my hand on the door of my packed car—my father said, Wait. He went into the garage, then emerged holding a wire cage in which two small, green birds were jailed. They were on sale, he said.

I drove with the cage buckled to the passenger seat. The relentless racket of the birds was like the panicked pitch of a tripped alarm. I was unable to tell whether it was directed toward me, toward one another, or toward the sky that passed above them out the window and the other birds they saw—if they saw them—strung on cables and perched on light posts, or else drifting in slow, aimless circles.

The smaller, uglier bird was the male. He tormented the female—unless she liked that kind of thing. He'd chew her neck and crowd her to a corner, where, if he could manage it, they'd fuck. When I refreshed their little dishes of seeds and water, he'd eat first—making a mess she'd clean up.

If I covered their cage with a heavy cloth, they went silent in the sudden dark and did not stir until I lifted it. To clear my head, I'd sometimes leave them cloaked for days. Then, flung without warning into cruel daylight—that was when I loved them most, if I ever loved them. I'd take the stunned, sedated female in hand. Her body looked plump, pliable, but felt hard, hollow. Under my thumb, her heart twitched.

Then she stopped eating, and soon I buried her beneath the arborvitae behind my building. The next morning, I crouched to where she lay headless on the dead grass. From a ground-level window, the landlord's fat white cat opened its mouth—a black cavern on a snowy hillside.

The little widower, the fresh bachelor—I stood in front of his cage. Wildly he climbed the bars. He wanted to blind me—he was blunt about it with his body and his shrill speech. I offered my index finger. He clamped it hard, which hurt, but not as much as I'd thought it would.

A few years later, my parents died—one after the other—from speedy, unforeseen diseases. My sister—a stranger, twenty years my senior—drove from where she lived and loaded her car. She left me the house key. It hung from a fat pink dolphin fob. In a fun font, the fob said *Florida Is for Lovers.*

When I let myself in, there was a very still, sun-cooked smell in the house. I hung my jacket, wiped my shoes on the rug, and went to the marble-topped, mirror-backed cabinet where they kept their bottles and glasses. I offered myself a drink, which I accepted.

I took my tumbler of cognac to my mother's mohair reading chair. I plopped my legs onto *A History of English Country Houses*, which lay open on the ottoman. Her potted plants, I saw, would not last. I poured another drink and went upstairs.

In their bedroom, I opened Mother's lacquered stack of velvet-lined drawers. My sister took the aggressive jewels—the diamond shoulder dusters, the silver slave bracelets, the Italian choker. But here was a plain gold chain fixed to a locket with a photograph of a man—not my father—inside. Here was a thick copper ring set with a large black stone that streaked orange when I slipped it onto my finger.

My father's sport coat hung from a desk chair, the pockets stuffed with wads of ones and fives. On the desktop was an unfinished letter and a stubbed-out cigarette. In the bottommost drawer I found a tiny pistol with a pearl handle. It looked like a toy, and might have been.

Later I locked the house and drove to the apartment I shared with a man I'd met waiting for a bus. On the turnpike, I rolled my window down to toss the tumbler. It split on the pavement, then disappeared beneath the wheels of a big rig.

When I arrived, the apartment was dark. I took the ring from my finger and lifted the locket over my head. I unkinked the bills. I pulled the pistol from my pocket. I arranged everything in a neat line on the dining table.

He came up behind me and put his hands on my neck.

I've just robbed a place, I said.

Looks like there wasn't much to take, he said, squeezing me in a way I'd come—after many years of failed attempts—to enjoy.

MEN OF THE WOODS

THE FATHER

He was a sharpshooter in the war, but now did odd jobs like cutting up dead or dying trees or shoveling run-over animals from the road and driving them to where they were burned. He raised his son and they raised rabbits for meat. They did not eat the meat. He'd quit forcing the boy's mouth open. The boy wouldn't budge. To make the boy happy, he covered the rabbit cages with cloth when he drove them to market so the rabbits might think it was night, and sleep. But the rabbits hopped from side to side and trembled like always, which made it hard to tell what they thought.

THE SON

He nursed the rabbit kits with tepid droppers of fake milk and kept one or two warming in his shirt pockets while he watched television in his bedroom with the door locked. When he played with them he tried to be gentle, but it was hard. His body was big and loose and he couldn't get it to do anything lightly. One little rabbit he dropped on its head from his great height. One he squished beneath his heavy booted foot.

When the rabbits escaped into the woods, he went after them with a sack slung over his back. The rabbits sometimes died of natural causes, such as old age and fright. When that happened, he kindled a fire in the yard and placed the dead rabbits into it with care. Then he kneeled in the grass and watched the flames lick and fuss their fur like their mothers did.

THE BLACK-HAIRED BOY

He dug in his father's desk until he found a butterfly knife, a vial of pills, and a tied-up stack of letters his mother had written. He swallowed the pills with milk and lay in his father's recliner, where he read the letters and decided his mother was a useless woman. He went outside with the knife and stuck it into tree trunks and fence posts and anthills. He walked along the river and through the woods to the other side of town, where a girl named Jenny lived. He squatted in the bushes behind her house and looked.

Their lights were on and they were sitting down to supper, Jenny and her sister and brother and parents. Jenny's fat dog came sniffing up to the boy in the bushes, wagging its tail. The boy stood and undid his pants. He aimed his stream at the dog's head. The dog flinched, then barked, and the boy ran, stumbling—fumbling his parts and snaps—putting himself away as he went.

He lost his way back. He stood in the woods while the dark came down. He dropped his knife and never found it.

THE THIN BOY

His grandmother was very old and his mother was sick from her life, so they sat tethered in a blue spell on the sofa. The thin boy lay on the floor between them while the television jumped and shouted.

His grandmother's legs were turned to stone and his mother's were rapidly hardening. When the boy felt the stiff cold creeping, he sprang up and ran out the door.

He ran up the hills and down the dells of the farmer's pasture—the heads of the farmer's cows all rising to consider him. He ran along the road that went into town one way and away from it the other. He ran in the woods along the river. While he waited for the other boys to come home or come outside, he ran 'round and 'round their houses and ringed the grass limp.

THE BOYS

They sat on floors together moving their men. They beat the hard little bodies against each other until one of them broke.

Then the thin boy found a box of his mother's women. The men came molded in their clothes—their skin rigid, their hair all of a piece—but the women were strippable and their skin was prickable and their hair was grippable. The women were large—giants. Next to them, the men looked shrunken and strange with tiny, pinched faces and ineffectual little hands.

The boys cut and burned the women's hair and yanked off arms and legs. They gave a blond one to a dog. They buried the ugly ones behind the rabbit hutch and kept the pretty ones for torture and rescue plots.

THE WOODS

Its low-hanging branches stalled them. Its brambles clung to their shirts. It lay rotted logs in their way. It tore strands from their socks. It drew their blood. It drank their piss. It ate their shit. It hid the light of day. It hid the stars at night. It hid the path to town. It looked very similar from one place to the next.

THE FATHER

From the window over his kitchen sink, he watched the thin boy run and remembered what fast felt like. He had a bad leg and a general stiffening of his blood. His temperament had soured. His lugubrious days slogged on.

His boyhood mornings had been sharp and bright. They'd woken him like a poke. He would pack a sandwich and run to the woods. He'd stay all day. Home was no place to be. He watched the ducks and deer and squirrels and song-birds. He wanted to touch them all—so he brought his rifle. His breath was steady and his aim was true. Afterward, he kneeled and laid a hand on the warm body until it cooled. The bodies taught him the important things of life.

But first, he learned to sit quiet and still and long. He could stop his breath. He could stop his heart. He could be a stone, a piece of wood, a leaf.

Only then would things start to stir. From where they'd hidden themselves, all of the rare, careful animals would rise—slowly, warily, testing the air—even the lonesome men who spent their days crouched among the thorny shrubs and rough, wild grasses.

SMALL PINK FEMALE

I've courted in the traditional fashion, of course—coming together on evenings arranged in advance, in the dark, on padded seats, facing the brash rectangle, or else in simulated candlelight with knees beneath a drooping white cloth, enduring protracted sessions of mastication and, later, abbreviated fornication.

Then, on a fine afternoon—sprung loose from any duty or thought—I found myself in the far corner of a florist's shop, sniffing around. From behind an enormous pittosporum emerged a small pink female, neatly aproned. I let her lead me to her chilled case of product. Here were entities that had unfurled slowly, elongated steadily—until severed.

The odor of that place—it did something to me. I love you, I said, handing her all of my money. I walked stiffly out the door, clutching the cold bundle to my chest. From the bottom, it leaked gently onto my arm.

Later, in private, I undid the wrapping and gazed at the gangly splay across my table. Some positioning was necessary—as well as some trimming, pinching, plucking, and shoving—to reveal their best advantage.

I did glimpse her once more—little, bulbous, waddling slightly ahead of me, her hair like a toasted dinner roll on the back of her head—and I ran forward gasping, spraying my face with spittle. I flung a wild arm and spun her by the shoulder and dropped to my knees, grabbing a plump hand. Please! I shouted. I'd never been happier.

But I've made bad choices from the start—ask any of my associates. In my temperate apartment, the heads relaxed one by one—then burst in fits of yellow dander. And oh, how quickly they shriveled then—falling limply as wads of used tissue, issuing no scent whatever.

POWER TOOLS

He lights his lawn on fire once a year. He does his weeding on hands and knees, with a knife. The neighborhood is dense and suburban, the freeway and airport just adjacent, but in cool months has a northwoods smell, a frontier kind of aroma, because he heats his house with a woodstove. He scavenges the wood and prepares it with a chainsaw early mornings. The chainsaw enters our dreams, then breaks them into wakefulness.

On certain nights he lights his homemade fireworks. They sizzle, flare. Some, inevitably, are duds.

He rides an old bicycle with a milk crate tied to the back, which he fills with things he finds on the ground. His house he built by hand, from scrap, piece by piece by piece. Still, he can never decide whether the ground objects are things found or things lost. Does he live in a found house or a lost one?

When the scales tip toward lost, he spends all night emptying his drawers, his garage, lugging a bulging sack through the streets.

Every so often he sleeps under the overpass, to see what it's like.

Animals come for the food he scatters on his grass. They skulk at night, their backs arched in contempt. Their lamp-green eyes wink from his trees. He learns their language. His deep-freeze fills with shrink-wrapped meat in a spectrum of pink.

The bones he cleans into gleaming white abstractions. He puts them in mailboxes and planters, on downspouts and stoops.

The police come to his home and take him away. The crime is understood to be either: (a) possession of bomb-building supplies; (b) possession of marijuana and/or hallucinogenic drugs; (c) growing marijuana plants in a windowless basement room; (d) possession of child pornography; or (e) child molestation.

A few days later, he returns in a taxi. He stands for hours in his yard, arms folded like he's cold.

The shriek of his saw reaches out to every house in the neighborhood. It comes in whether windows are open or shut. It interrupts the interior sounds of television and radio, washing machine and dishwasher—interrupts even the thoughts of the occupants. It disturbs the electricity of their brains in such a way, to such a degree, that they are unable to determine whether or not the sound is coming from outside their heads.

SHH

My surgeon's two big purebreds, Buck and Geoff, led incredible lives. They ate top-shelf meat, delivered daily and ground by hand by the housekeeper. To simulate the stomach contents of small prey animals like rabbits and squirrels, the housekeeper included scant plant matter, some fruit. When my surgeon and his wife traveled, they picked resorts that catered to canine luxury: spa treatments, fine dining, elite sports.

My surgeon gave considerable sums—enough, by the sound of it, to support several sizable families—to animal rights groups. His wife was very particular about their leather. She rescued wrecked racehorses—doomed for glue—to keep as pets.

And when moles mangled his neighbor's matchless lawn,

my surgeon slapped the neighbor on the back and said, *Live and let live, Al—what's so bad about a few lumps in the grass?*

But then my surgeon discovered an invasion of mice in the climate-controlled garage where he kept his classic car collection. These were very special, very expensive cars, regularly loaned for films and magazines. The mice devoured the hoses of several engines. They soiled the seats and left dribbles and droppings along dashboards. In the glovebox of his prized Porsche, a mother mouse birthed a litter of pups.

The exterminator recommended glue traps. I didn't think it through, my surgeon said. He shook his head sadly. The next morning he found them—cruelly stuck, alive, crying.

What did you do? I said. I was flat on my back below him, gowned and shaved.

Well, he said, I got my bag. I got my scalpel. I thought I could slice them off of there. They'd have clumps of glue on their feet, but they'd be free, he said.

Did it work? I said. Did you save them? A nurse fitted a mask on my face. Someone turned on the gas.

Well, no, he said. The first one I tried, I sliced off its foot instead. There was a lot of blood, actually. It was terrible, he said.

I opened my mouth, but only a little squeak came out.

Shh, said the surgeon. Over my face, his gloved hand hung—you could even say it twitched. Then, with his fingertips, he pushed the lids of my eyes shut. You've seen this move before—some man, overcome with shame, unable, for selfish reasons, to look at what he's done.

MOTHER'S TEETH

Brenda, Mother said—I can't find my teeth!

So I checked her ornate nightstand, her pedestal sink, and the little glass table near the big iron chair on her private patio where dry bougainvillea blossoms piled like pink paper party favors. Mother followed me with her walker, saying, Do you see them? Where could they be?

They were not in her hutch of collectible china or her cabinet of costly curios. They were not in the closet where she kept the expensive clothes she wore. They were not in the closet where she kept the more expensive clothes she did not wear. They were not in the small, sodden bag of garbage beneath the kitchen sink or in the garage, in the larger bin of garbage that smelled like the corpse of an animal.

I came back to the dining room, where she sat with a cup

of coffee. Slowly, she brought the cup to her mouth, took a sip—then curled her lip. She looked up at me.

Brenda, she said, do you suppose they're in my mouth? She opened it wide—and there they were.

After that we rushed over to the hospital, where Mother was late for her chemotherapy appointment.

A nurse brought us to a room dimmed by dark blinds, crammed with chairs. In each one sat a person attached to a sack of clear liquid that drained down a tube into the person's arm. The nurse lightly smacked Mother until her vein stood up to receive. Within a few minutes, Mother was asleep. It took four hours for the liquid to drain fully into someone.

I took her purse from her lap and drove to the recreational facility that looked like a coliseum. In the middle, rather than a gladiatorial arena, was a large, round swimming pool. I made a big splash. I pushed to the bottom of the deep end, where I sat quietly, emitting little bubbles.

On a yellow chaise longue I dried myself. A group of elderly men were sunning their bodies nearby. Soon one of them got up and came to stand above me. He had a rigid torso and skin like baked bread, tufted all over with wiry white fluff.

I've never seen you before, he said.

Just visiting, I said.

I'd be happy to give you the grand tour, he said. He lifted his arms high, like he was holding the sky. Heaven on earth! he said.

I fucked him in a stall in the ladies' locker room. You look just like my daughter Jackie, he said, panting.

I put my clothes back on over my suit and drove to the grocery store, where it was approximately forty-five degrees Fahrenheit inside. On Mother's card I charged a hand of green bananas, a gallon of orange juice, some mixed nuts in a red netted bag, and a tub of pistachio ice cream.

At Mother's condo, I ate the ice cream from the tub with a large spoon. It had been whipped in a way to make it very airy. It scooped itself in soft, generous green slabs and dripped onto the speckled countertop—a garish variety of pinkish granite that looked like vomit.

Where were you? Mother said when I got back to the hospital. I'm so cold, she said. I'm really hungry, she said. I got her to the car and drove to Rita's. Mother sat in back, looking out the window.

I was just thinking about that time you were supposed to watch your brother, she said. When he almost drowned. Do you remember that?

She ordered the egg plate with hash brown potatoes, sausage links, white toast with jelly, and fruit cocktail. Her insurance covered the chemo that doesn't make you sick to your stomach, which was much more expensive than the one that does. It let her keep her hair, too—a thick headful she set in hot rollers and wrapped in a cap when she showered.

My daughter would like to order something, too, Mother said.

I'm fine, I said to Rita. Thank you.

She'll have the egg plate, Mother said.

I don't want the egg plate, I said to Rita.

What's wrong with the egg plate? It's delicious, Mother said.

I'm sure it is, I said to Rita. All of your dishes look very appetizing.

She'll have the egg plate, Mother said.

Mother ate everything, then used her toast to wipe up. She looked at me. She looked at my egg plate. We're not leaving until you eat that, she said.

I've got no place to be, I said.

◆

The sun was setting when Mother woke up from her nap. I'm hungry, she said.

Alone, I drove past the hamburger place, the pizza parlor, the sub shop. I stopped at a Thai restaurant in a strip mall.

There was a pair of large gold elephant statues that greeted you when you came in. I passed beneath a jeweled curtain to the hostess station and ordered two shrimp pad thais to go, then went back outside to wait. The sky was a ridiculous pink, dotted over with little shreds of purple cloud like a torn-up letter. The palms were doing their slow wag in the wind. Heat rose from the concrete as from a radiator. It was six o'clock, but it seemed everyone had gone to bed.

Back at the condo, I dumped our noodles from their foam boxes onto plates. Mother chewed each bite a long time, looking thoughtfully at the food, her head slightly tilted to one side. She picked up a large shrimp with her chopsticks and carefully bit off the head end. When she'd swallowed it, she looked at the rest of the body, then at me. What sort of chicken is this? she said.

After that I helped her up, and in the bathroom we put her teeth in a jar of sanitizing solution. Without them, her face collapsed a little—it was alarming. But if you didn't know her, you might just think that was how she looked—soft, sick, sad-mouthed, old.

She got into bed, where she lay on her back and pulled the blanket up to her chin. Goodnight, Brenda, she said.

Here she was—the woman who made me eat until I puked, then made me eat the puke. *Wendell always was oversexed*—that's what she said when I told her what my father did. And when she found me playing in the place we dumped our garbage out back, she picked up a chunk of glass and cut my hand open with it. *Brenda*, she'd said, *this is what happens when you play in the garbage. Understand?*

But now she is dead and I am rich because everything she owned is mine, which—in my understanding—is the best possible outcome for this story.

THE BABY

They have the baby out of doors today. They are all out there together, gathered around it. I've seen it once and am picturing it now as they talk—its very dark and large, startled eyes and amusing hair. I will grant it is a good-looking baby, unless its looks have already shifted, as often happens with these creatures so barely and newly alive, which may help explain my reluctance to hold one in my arms—their heads, after all, are soft and malleable as a peach!

I can't see to know what they're doing, and their language is a different one than mine. Their laughter rolls up over my fence, through the flowering trees, up the uneven steps and through the screens of the house, which are crossed with metal bars. The family is doing something to the baby, that much is clear—they are provoking it for their own enjoyment.

The baby is difficult to figure. It sounds like a nest of squirrels I found after a storm. One of them had died in the fall from the tree, and the other two chattered next to it, to me, as though to tell me of their trouble. I understand the inappropriateness of comparing a human baby to a squirrel baby. I don't know why I continue to do so. I cannot help it that a human baby also reminds me of an overfull helium balloon hovering too close to a hot bulb.

PLEASE

I went alone to the pagan museum and to the historic
fountain because he'd been unable to defecate since we'd
arrived nearly a week prior. When I returned at dinnertime
he held a baguette in one hand and a hank of salami in the
other, tearing a bite from each before speaking. I can force it
out this way, he said.

His face was very red and he was sweating, but I washed a
glass and poured him a beer and we sat on the terrace drinking until it was time to lie down—though the regular resi-
dents of that place were just waking up.

He rejected medicine of any kind—believed in the body
and its mechanisms. He competed regularly in lengthy events
of strenuous activity, and could lift me off the ground with
one hand in his pocket.

Nonetheless, when I awoke, he'd bound himself in the bedsheets and he was breathing in a heavy, smacking way.

I prepared the coffee and on a small plate arranged carefully washed fruits. Soon he set his cup down, sloshing the coffee over the rim in his excitement, and hurried to the bathroom.

He picked up the cup from its puddle when he came out and shook his head sadly—though by then the coffee had gone cold, and he would not drink cold coffee.

I might have envied his predicament, since whatever I swallowed made its swift and irritable trip from one end to the other, resulting in daily harassment. In a similar manner, I rush from one situation to the next, often arriving too quickly.

Yet, I could sit in a restaurant and request of the waiter some water and plain vegetables, please, and be understood. A little heap of the vegetables on a plate would arrive a few minutes later—lightly steamed, steaming still—accompanied by a small cup of oil or melted butter for dipping or drizzling, though most often I ate them unadorned between sips of water.

I went on to collect pamphlets and paused to read plaques of note. In one plaza people had been bound and set alight—alive—by their fellow citizens. In another, shoppers had been trampled by a large herd of animals.

Later, at the entrance to a park, I stood before a pair of pillars topped with a pair of heads—a man's and a woman's whose noses had been chipped to snubs—and on the woman's crown of cold braids was a pigeon, releasing from its under-carriage a loose white drib that slid down the woman's cheek like a teardrop.

◆

Back at the apartment, I found him slumped in a chair—pasty and waxen—and not wishing to talk.

Could I walk without toppling? Would I make it in time to relieve myself?

How funny—how funny—the baring of ass—how good to sit.

There then came an angry banging on the door. But it was the hot hiss I was listening to—the miraculous stream—unaided, unbeckoned—of what had so recently been lolling around in my mouth.

When at last I opened the door, he was standing right there, as if roused from a spell. A clump—oily and black—was on the floor.

I made it, he said—casting a proud look down upon it and upon me—and for dinner I'll have some soft yellow cheese.

BAIT-AND-SWITCH

We rented it by loophole. It had a wood-paneled rumpus room, a pink claw-foot tub, a tire swing in the yard, beige Berber wall-to-wall. The kitchen was papered in a repeating print of beribboned geese. It was like the house of some scrubbed friend whose parents fussed a sleepover—presenting bowls of name-brand snacks and a bland stack of video rentals.

We hauled in our resinous heaps and spread them haphazardly throughout the rooms. We smoked in the tub—ashed into the sink—puked the shower. We stored our liquor in the large linen closet that smelled sweetly of the clean bedding of a clean family at first—and then of the sour, sticky rings our bottles left.

We had a party. We bought twenty pounds of wings, three kegs of beer. When we dumped out the keg tub sludge in the yard, we found the pizza cutter, three forks, two steak knives, sixteen chicken bones, a gold hoop earring, and eighty-five cents in change at the bottom. We left the items spread across the grass until the grass grew over them.

Then—in the fall—they arrived. They came for the food we left dribbled on countertops and shattered across floors, loosely bagged in cupboards and drawers, and crusted in slicks on plates on our bedside stands. We found them in the kitchen, breakfasting on our toaster crumbs. We found them nested in our odorous shoes. They roamed freely—unafraid— procreating, manducating, urinating, and defecating.

We bought traps and stretched them. We cut up candy bars and placed the chunks gently. With two fingers we pinched the carcassed traps and carried them to the trash bin.

Then we laid the bait that made them sick slowly. They crawled off to die in the walls where we couldn't reach them. They died in the air ducts. When we switched on the furnace, the sweet, heated stink of rot pushed from the grates.

They were cannibals. We found bodies—poisoned by us—the brains eaten from the skulls like soup from a bowl.

That's fucked-up, he said.

Then one night he came home to our dark room. He reeked of spirits and of smoke. He took off his clothes, got into bed, lit a cigarette. He jumped, he yelled—he flung one from him. We saw it hit the wall—a soft thump. We watched it drop to the floor—still.

He picked up his cigarette from where it had fallen and walked to the wall, saw the thing was not dead—just stunned.

He sprayed the body with a can of paint, then put it in a plastic bag, tied the bag shut, and left the room.

Through the window, I saw him outside—unclothed, smoking his cigarette—tossing the bag into the frozen yard. Then he came back and dropped his cigarette into a can of beer on the floor. He got into bed and put his hand on my middle.

No mercy, he said.

Soon, he took off my clothes. We heard a staccato of springs snapping, of necks breaking.

His regular techniques included the foot-in-the-door, the door-in-the-face, the low-ball, and the bait-and-switch—all of which I allowed.

THE IMPRECATION

A day after she died, the man came to cut the broken air-conditioning unit from the wall. The back end of the unit hung outside, beneath a messy tree. When the man pulled the unit through the hole into the house, dry leaves and little twigs and dirt and squirrel droppings and oblong pods fell all over the floor.

The man carried the old unit out the front door and down to the curb. The hole in the wall brightened the small, dim room—there was a fresh, cheerful feeling. A sense of serenity came from some glowing, floating dust.

But then the man came back and jammed the new unit into the hole. He turned it on with a remote control. Within a few minutes the room was cool, but it couldn't help her because she was dead.

For three weeks I'd poured cold water on her in the tub

and set her in front of a floor fan. I'd held her up to the open freezer and pressed ice cubes under her arms until they melted. I'd squirted water into her mouth with a little rubber bulb I used to irrigate my ears. But I'd also wrapped her in thick blankets later, when she started to shiver. I'd hugged and rubbed her until she fell asleep. I kept my hand on her side, which rose and fell with effort.

When she died, I helped lift her body into a box to be carried away. Unlike the ugly, busted air conditioner the man took to the curb, her small, old body was clean and soft and looked useful still—still with life in it, something not yet ready to be thrown out or, in this case, burned.

For three weeks the man said he would come, but did not come. Now he'd come and expected a hero's welcome, but because she was dead, I no longer cared whether the room was hot or cold.

I got the broom and swept the mess he'd made. When it was piled, I saw that among the leaves and twigs and pods were little clumps of her white hair. I kneeled and carefully removed them from the dirt.

I did not thank the man when he left. He was a businessman, self-made and busy, with many irons in the fire. He was tasked daily with assorted problems of greater and lesser importance—the broken air conditioner, for example, being a very low priority—but one sensed he got a great deal of enjoyment from his life. His trendy eyeglasses he pushed to the top of his head while he worked, and his casual clothes were of a particular, pricey type. He whistled and checked his phone often, apparently invigorated by how much he was needed.

I stood at the window with her hair in my hand. I closed my fingers around it. I could hear her breath near my ear, though I'd heard her breath stop. My insides haven't worked right since. Not my brain, either.

I watched the man drive away in his glossy, valuable car and prayed he might be met with some misfortune. Due to a major failing—the pathological poverty of my imagination—I could not call to mind anything more specific than that.

DEAR SIRS

The first time I saw your products, I could not help but shout. They brought me joy and I felt exclusively warm from them. I thought how good it would be to look at them every day in the comfort of my home, which is maybe not as comfortable as one would like—especially one accustomed to the great comforts you doubtless possess—but for me it is comfortable enough, and because I do not move around much, its smallness does not impinge on me the way it would impinge on you, Sirs.

You might think my home too small to contain even a single one of your products, but I assure you I have taken pains to clear a space within which the full excellence of your items will be easily apprehended by all who look on them, though I rarely entertain guests and it will most likely be myself only

who feasts his eyes. But a man must have his private pleasures, mustn't he?

I said to myself, You cannot bring these into your home
without first preparing for them a good place, a nice place. You
would not bring home a new baby before you'd made for it a
little bed laid with soft blankets and something special for it
to look at, something you've hung from the ceiling to catch
the light of the sun, because you know babies need this type
of enchantment. And so I have worked hard and made many
sacrifices, but now the day has finally come.

My problem, Sirs—and the reason I write to you this
morning—is that I cannot find my country. Where my country
should rightfully reside—alphabetically speaking—I find only
the country before it and the country after. I see the names of
many other countries, some great—the very best ones. Yours,
for example, good Sirs. But there are lesser countries, too—
many, even, that are very bad. I hope you will not think me
too bold when I say that my country—small though it may
be—is far superior to many of these. And yet, they are there
and we are not.

Is it because of our smallness we cannot be found? Are we
so small you have forgotten us?

If you have forgotten us—an oversight I comprehend
easily as a servant in a clerical capacity, tasked daily with
many a trivial detail and forever failing to remember some
item of little import to myself yet significant, even gravely so,
to another party—I say, if indeed you have forgotten us, I here
humbly submit my request.

At your earliest convenience, and barring any compre-
hensible reason as to why you would not, might you attend
to—nay, rectify—the situation as outlined above, in which
I, together with my countrymen—a good and clean people
we—have been made to wait, so many of us, until you deem
it appropriate?

COLONIAL REVIVAL

He came back from the war with a little bit of money and the helmet of a man he killed with a knife in the charred husk of a house. With the money he opened a small shop crafting fine reproductions of antique furniture. He was a competent craftsman but a better overseer—his business grew quickly once he replaced himself with several young woodworkers.

He was fond of horses. He wore his shiny riding boots while striding the aisles of his factory—for it quickly became a small factory—and when he found a wife, he bought her a big gray mare as a wedding gift. She didn't care for horses— their smell or expense or the sounds they made. She preferred cats and collected as many as six or seven at a time—rare breeds with long hair, malformed faces, and bad temper- aments. She traveled to nearby cities and towns in her big black sedan to display them, sometimes returning with purple or yellow or green satin ribbons, which she hung on the walls of the guest cottage where the cats lived.

He appointed the big main house himself, before they met. It was done in a fine colonial revival style, furnished entirely with the products of his factory. The wallpaper imitated a homely, hand-painted pattern. He found an Amish woman to weave his curtains. In the evening he and his wife would sit by the brick hearth in a pair of oak rocking chairs and watch the sun set through the collection of antique glass bottles he'd arranged in the west-facing windows.

In addition to the show cats and gray mare, many other animals came and went, dogs and parakeets and barn cats and different horses—and they had several children, too.

When the children left, his wife's body began dismantling her from inside out. When she was too ill to have intercourse with her husband, she found a kind woman who was willing to do it for her.

After his wife died, the man continued to have intercourse with the kind woman until she, too, died. Then he spent most of his time alone until his son appeared on his doorstep one day, carrying a dirty cloth sack of belongings, asking to be let in for supper.

The man learned to cook as a soldier and could do several dishes serviceably. He broke some eggs in a pan and tended them while his son sat at the table looking at his hands. His son's face was thin and tired and old. It was strange to have an old man for a son. He did not like to look at his son's face.

He put his son in what had once been the boy's bedroom. Now it was crowded with the man's factory office—his impressive desk, his files and drawings, his dainty models of chairs and chifforobes. The taste for his product had gone sour in the public's mouth long ago. What they wanted now was the look of wood but not the price. They wanted to pitch everything to the curb for new every few years.

When he closed the factory, he'd built a big steel building at the south corner of his property and filled it with what inventory remained. To take the air in the afternoons he would walk there, crossing his lawn and the long, fenced pasture. He'd unbolt the heavy lock and stick his head inside.

The building was windowless, unelectrified. The dark had a watchful quality. For days, his workers had trundled in and out, scrambled up and down, shouting and sweating, stacking everything into a pile that reached the ceiling. The uppermost pieces had threatened to tip the whole but now sat serene.

The man squinted. There was a leg—there an arm. There were empty seats, empty chests. But unlike others he'd seen, this was a bloodless tangle. The smell of it all drifted up to him—cool, dry, bottled. The man breathed deeply through his nose. Without the smell, there were many things he forgot.

THE LOCKET

Under a noon sun, on a black cloth, lay a glitter of metal—
hard to look at. I picked up a locket—old, gold—and
dangled it by its chain. I wedged my nail in its seam and split
it open like a piece of fruit.

Inside was a man from the neck up. He wore a white collar and a black coat and he had a head full of rich hair. His
face was stiff as stone beneath the glass, but I could see how it
might move. It seemed to me he'd been thinking of a woman
when the photographer ducked beneath his dark cloak.

Maybe the man cut his face out and applied paste to the
back. Maybe he pressed it in, snugged the glass, shut the
dome—then fixed the clasp to the woman's neck. Let's hope
he lifted her hair so as not to snare it. Let's hope he lowered
his lips there. On her nape, from the chain, the woman felt a
light, cold, creeping prick.

The locket shone like a small sun before it dulled into something more earthbound. When it slid across the woman's skin, she thought of the man inside. Sometimes she moved just to feel it.

I walked home with the thing tangling in my pocket. When I arrived, the locket was warm as my thigh.

I worked as a mail clerk at a warehouse that cut small discs of tin. All day long the pieces rained ringing down the chutes. The air tasted sour and sharp like blood when you opened your mouth. The man who ran operations had skin that flushed red while he worked. His arms were covered in coarse yellow hair that caught the silver shavings as they fell like sparks from the machines.

I'd stand at my station, sorting. He'd walk past with a speed that disturbed my clothes—my skirt a sweep of fingertips, my shirt a hand that traveled up my back. My hair lifted and sighed into place again.

The letters lay limp while I listened for his step. It seemed I could hear the smallest sound from a great distance. When I drove home in the evening, I took the long way through dried-up fields. I found dependable pleasure in the yield of the gas pedal to my foot. The life in me—it always pulsed harder the closer it came to its end.

THE HUNGRY VALLEY

The old horse had hobbled hooves and a doubled middle because the man fed it too much rich corn. The old dog's back was broad and thin of hair like a threadbare piece of overstuffed furniture, yet the man continued to drizzle its kibble with bacon grease. The cats lapped milk he poured into pie tins on the barn floor and they ate the rats that ate the sacks of rich corn, so they, too—the cats as well as the rats—were quite fat.

On the dog's ears, ticks sucked themselves big as grapes. Burly black flies drank from the flanks of the horse. Mosquitoes and fleas got their blood meal from the most convenient body.

When the veterinarian gelded the horse—quickly, with a corroded blade—the man sat on the horse's head. Then the vet tossed what he'd cut to the man's dogs—different ones then, who fought over the hot, wet heap.

The man's children, when they were children, carried the cats like sacks of grain and dressed them in doll clothes. They watched the slick births of the kittens. Once, when they touched a litter too early, the mother ate the kittens in front of them—four soft bodies gulped whole.

Behind the man's house was a pond. Early evenings, he cast a line into it. He hooked little fish with worms, then chopped them into bait for bigger fish, which he boned, gutted, beheaded, and fried.

He'd hunted the deer—made stew and jerky of them—but now he watched them from his armchair with a blanket on his knees. The deer forgot to be afraid and grazed brazenly on the lawn.

In the kitchen were his wife's honed blades and copper cookware, her coddled crockery and polished cutlery—but the man, alone, used only an old cast-iron skillet, a flimsy tin fork, and a camping knife. His humble cookery tended toward scalded. While he ate, he tried to conjure his wife's elegant preparations, but there was only the perpetual smell of burnt meat.

After his children left and before his wife found a large, hard lump in her thigh, the man rode the gelding daily, at dusk, to his property's boundary and back. They'd round the pond and cut through the woods, past the collapsed house where a pastor's family perished by fire in a prior century.

At the top of the ridge, the valley yawned wide. Willingly, they walked into it.

One night, coming back, the gelding grunted, then

bolted. The man struggled to stay seated as the horse crashed through the brush. Then he saw the reason—four coyotes flanked them. Their mouths hung open. They looked at the man as they ran. They seemed to take some measure of him.

The man's house appeared on the hilltop—every window lit. In the kitchen, his wife stood at the sink, washing. When the man looked down again, the coyotes were gone.

At dinner, his wife was excited. The man smiled but got up from his unfinished plate to stand at the window. When the witchy yipping of the pack began, he strained to see but could not get past his own face in the glass.

Before bed, she sat brushing her hair. Her husband rarely shared anything fearful—she was happy.

But later she woke to a wailing she recognized. The raw cry—it gripped her. It dragged her from bed, down the hall, out the door. She walked quickly toward it, her arms stretched straight ahead. Like the cramp of a lost leg, she felt the old burden of milk in her chest.

For a while she could be seen in her white nightgown, but then the dark—it swallowed her.

VICTORIAN WEDDING PORTRAIT

His intentions seemed very good, but often balked when harnessed. He could speak intelligently about a number of subjects, but most often he wandered the field alone. Nothing to be done: he would always be easier with men than with women. Recall the story of the poor girl-child playmate—reviled, ridiculed. Disfigured by a pot of ink.

By the time his bride arrived, he'd memorized his cloak-and-dagger act. His soft, swift assurance swooned her—but only an hour. No fool she, and no half-lidded maneuverings escaped her. She, too, loved power and its intoxication.

She developed a dappled scarlet rash and used it as a passport. When at last it seemed no more good could come, she collapsed into a sweat and the doctor was called. He diagnosed an acute consumption of nerve. She played at it until the last drop had been wrung, then pulled on her boots for a romp.

On he went, scaling the summits and slaying the beasts that blocked his way. His diligence became a mania, then a specter. Taller grew the stacks of paper, vaster the horizon of his daily riding-out. Creature comforts made him itch. He tried his best regarding the flannel pajamas, the bedside jar of flowers, and damply conciliatory jokes—it was the right thing to do. But alas! In this life, to what do we pin our badges?

The efficiency of their machine astonished and delighted passersby and the dogs at the hearth. No respite for it, but they applied oil to the joints religiously. It was passed to their children in a velvet-lined case: a timepiece, an instrument, a weapon, a relic.

B J

Never mind his head was too small for his body—he was big and handsome, broad of chest, with dark hair that grew in thick luxury and was a pleasure to comb. Mealtime was what we looked forward to. When I was sloppy with my plate, I could count on him to help. When we were done, I'd sit on the floor and he'd lay his full weight on me and groan as he did so. I'd wrap one arm around his neck and squeeze.

Then, when I came home early from work one day, he was on the porch of a neighbor's house with several children attending to him. They'd made a wreath for his head and a garland for his neck and around him lay several small bundles of grass and sticks as well as a large, dirty cow bone and a bright orange ball and the shrunken, naked bodies of some synthetic men and women.

I stopped and rolled down my window. I shouted. He

cringed—caught!—then stood and shook off his accoutrements. He jumped into the back of the car and licked my ear.

Bye, BJ! a child shouted.

How do you know his name? I said.

Everybody knows BJ, the child said.

BJ was a slow stroller, a leisure-taker, a smeller of roses and corpses. Like a female, he'd gracefully squat to wet some bush or other. He never needed restraint. I'd loop his leash around my own neck instead. I liked the rhythmic thump of the clasp on my chest. I thought of a girl I knew who buckled a collar of black leather, studded with spikes, tight to her white throat.

For years he and I shared a happy home—I didn't worry. I'd work long hours and arrive home late, yet he was always happy to see me. Did I ignore the depressed expression he sometimes wore? Why didn't I wonder when he'd suddenly be soft and scented with lavender, as though he'd just had a bath?

On a damp Tuesday, he was gone. I put on my leash and went out, shouting his name. Finally, I came to a little white house with red shutters and potted pink petunias on the porch. A woman was on her hands and knees on the lawn. She shoved a spade beneath a weed, then lifted the clotted, rooty clump and dumped it in a bucket. BJ was behind her—his face deep in a large bowl.

Why are you feeding my dog? I asked the woman. She stopped her work to look at me.

She shrugged. He comes here every day, she said. He's always hungry.

He gets plenty to eat at home, I said. Please don't feed him. As you can see, he has a weight problem.

You sound like my ex, she said.

BJ, I called. Here, boy.

BJ? the woman said. That doesn't suit him at all. I call him Jonathan.

BJ, I said, let's go. But he either did not hear or did not care and continued to eat. I took the leash from my neck, pushed the clasp open. Where is his collar? I said.

Oh, I threw it away, she said.

This little woman turned out to be much stronger than she looked, and I to be weaker than I'd thought, and the taste of the mud and weeds she jammed into my mouth while we rolled in her yard was not as bad as you'd expect.

Meanwhile, he didn't look up, and he never came back.

Later, when I got my new job, I had to drive past the little white house with the red shutters and pink petunias every day—there was no other way—and although I would remind myself of what a big boss I was now, nonetheless, there they'd be, the two of them, out there together on the lawn, basking in a love like the biggest fuck-you yet seen.

COOLLY, BLUELY

When we got in I found the bathroom first, but she was at the door by the time I sat down.

I have to go to the bathroom, she yelled, pounding.

So do I, I said.

I really need to go, she said, jerking the knob.

When I finished, I picked a citrus scent from the soap heap and peeled it slowly, humming.

They were already in the bedroom with the door shut. Our things were slumped in a pile on the ground. I pulled the food from the sacks and stacked it on the shelves.

I'm hungry, she said, coming in.

Eat this, I said, and set a box in front of her.

She was busy a while unwrapping and chewing, looking out the window over the sink into the dark.

There was a peculiar smell about the place. The walls

were wooden but sealed with some glaring, shining coating. The furnishings had a look of bloat, with scarcely a pathway through. On the convertible sofa—our bed—lay a large quilt in chipper imitation of an antique, as though the past was a simpleminded child to pat on the head. The fabric felt stiff, resistant—like it might melt if put to flame.

We woke late but not a sound came from behind their door, so I cooked some eggs we ate from paper plates on our legs on the deck. The other cabins were closer than they'd looked in the dark. On an adjacent deck, a small boy dropped dry, bright cereal bits into the gape of his drawstring trousers. His mouth was open as if to cry, but no sound came.

We stuffed our totes and climbed a sandy path to the main road—a two-lane highway loud with trucks. Other people walked with foam noodles and dull towels that limped along the ground. We fell with them into a shuffle that broke apart when the shine of the water burst suddenly through the trees.

The sun made its arc overhead. It came red through our eyelids and sucked us dry. On the shore, we tried to lie still, but the creep of our skin—from the legs of insects or their mouths, probing, or the shrinking twitch of our limbs, burning—jostled us until we sat up in groggy irritation. We shielded our eyes. The lake was brown and warm as piss though it glittered coolly, bluely. The stinking muck of the bottom clung to our feet.

We needed water, sandwiches, antiseptic ointment, and a dim place to lie quietly awhile, but when we got back they'd locked us out. We beat on the windows of their bedroom.

Inside, the coil of bedding slumped to the floor. Pieces of clothing were flung. Next to the empty bed, the piled ashtray spilled. Bottles lay hollow on their sides.

We had a little bit of money between us, so we heaved our bags onto the deck and went back up to the road. We walked toward town this time, against traffic. We didn't look into the windows of the cars as they passed, but we could feel the looking coming out at us.

The town was built when the people at the bottom of the mountain had money to spend, and would come up for the summers to breathe the air. The buildings had an alpine aesthetic—degraded by age. There was an Irish pub, a sports bar, a carry-out liquor store, a smoking paraphernalia shop, and a country café that was already closed for the day. In the café's windows sat dusty baskets of nylon flowers and shattered husks of insects. The rest of the storefronts were empty. Their worn signs suggested a forgotten taste for cured meats and collectible china.

At the liquor store, we could afford a soda, a package of crackers, and a sack of sour candy worms. We squatted against the wall outside and counted out the pieces. We passed the bottle between us and took measured drinks.

Across the street, outside the sports bar, two men were smoking. They spoke loudly, striking the air for emphasis, and paused often to spit.

A woman was coming down the hill toward them. She moved like an old or injured person but wore bright, youthful clothing. Her hair was soft and orange on her shoulders.

When she reached the men, she stopped. One of them spit, then said something to the other. They laughed.

The woman turned away. She stumbled, then walked into the street without checking for traffic. A car approached, braked hard, and honked, but she didn't seem to see it. The car swerved angrily and sped up the hill.

When she stood in front of us, we saw that her eyes were very blue and loose, and that one hand quaked gently at her side.

You girls, she said after a minute. What have you got?

We held up our crumpled wrappers, the empty bottle, and shook our heads. She nodded. She drew a hand slowly across her nose, which was dripping. When the hand came away, it was smeared with red.

Dark came quickly—a darker dark than we knew. We followed the blue road back from town. We tripped on rocks and bottles on the shoulder. We held our arms up against the headlights that kept coming. We heard the sound of a window rolling down, a voice calling out. But we couldn't hear what was said, or didn't understand—and besides, it wouldn't be them out looking for us—so we didn't listen. We didn't think to glance back, didn't wonder who was speaking or what was wanted, didn't imagine anything worth stopping for at all.

LINE

I stand behind a woman much shorter than I am. The top of the back of her head reaches my collarbone, though I'm not tall. I'm of an average height. She has a lot of hair, voluminous and curly. Even oiled with some product to cohere it, her hair takes up so much room that I keep an extra foot between us out of respect. Sometimes when I ride the bus or train and I'm wearing my hair down, the person in the seat behind me touches or pulls it, by accident or not, when placing his hands on the handle on the back of my seat. When this happens I feel as though my hair should be tied up and netted instead of floating around for anyone to grab. So I keep my distance between myself and this woman's hair, but she keeps turning around to talk to a friend of hers behind me in line, and her hair brushes my forearm every time, soft and tickling like a hovering mosquito. When she turns the

third time, I read her shirt. She's wide, with breasts that prob-
ably give her backaches, and stretched taut across them, in
yellow letters: *Prepare to defend your chicken.* I glance back at
the woman's friend and the steadily lengthening line. Behind
me, a man with firmly folded arms, hands fisted into his arm-
pits, lifts his chin for a better look. A little girl leans against a
large box on the ground next to him, her shoulders limp, her
face turned to her feet, one hand bunching and twisting the
hem of her dress. The man glances sideways at the girl. I turn
forward again. He says, Huh? No, says the little girl. No? he
says. Yes, she says. No, she says. Yes, yes, yes, no, no, no, no, no.

DERLAND

He was two years older than I was and if I walked ahead of him on the stairs he would reach a hand up between my legs. If I forgot to lock the bathroom door, he would come in and ask—What are you doing?

He was the son of my uncle and a girl I never saw, and she was age of fourteen when baby Derland came out. Then baby Derland was brought into the home of my uncle and his wife Mildred and their two sons.

My uncle's name was Derland, too, but everyone except his wife called him Dick. She called him Derland and she called the boy Derland and when she called, *Derland! Stop what you're doing! Don't be so stupid!* it was hard to tell which Derland she meant.

Arranging flowers was Aunt Mildred's special talent. People came to her when they needed something pretty for a luncheon or a funeral. When she married Uncle Dick, she made herself a tourniquet of love-lies-bleeding.

Aunt Mildred kept her hair twisted and pinned in a rigid lump on the back of her head, but when she released it, it came down past her buttocks—nearly to her knees—and was a coarse, dark gray like some pelts I've felt. It took her an hour to wash it. I would help her with the towels, wringing the wet out foot by foot. In fine weather she'd hang her head out the bathroom window to let the hair fall down the side of the house into the sun. When a breeze came, it lifted the hair straight out like a large, floating rug.

I saw her once—in her bedroom, on the floor, in her girdle—while Uncle Dick stood at the bureau in his suit and wingtips, sipping from a glass, reading from a folded newspaper. I saw her lean forward to reach for his foot, and I saw the foot toss the hand away like a small, vexing dog. Then, without looking up, he unbuckled himself.

Uncle Dick—he was always unbuckling. He unbuckled all across this great land of ours. Eventually he headed south of the border to continue his life's work, and was never heard from again.

Now Aunt Mildred and I have a little shop together in town. We keep a garden and a nice house. Our advice is regularly sought by members of the community. On weekends, we take turns baking something new for each other. More often than not, what we make turns out tender and moist, with an excellent crumb.

Back then, the boy Derland had a trick of hooking his

pinkies into the edges of his mouth and, with his other fingers, tugging down the corners of his eyes. It made a melting mask of his face. It was the face he made when I jammed my knee into him and pushed him down the cellar steps. It was the face, too—wherever it may have been—that I imagined on Uncle Dick's head.

THE DOMINANT ANIMAL

Years ago I had two dogs, one large and one small, and one day the large one killed the small one, though it took the small one a day or so to die. When it was over I wrapped her in a towel and dug a hole beneath a pine tree and set heavy stones on her body and covered her with dirt while the large dog sat at a distance watching me.

After that I hated the large dog though he seemed sorry for what he'd done. He and the small dog had been friends. I refused to pet him even when he slipped his head under my hand hanging loose at my side. I wouldn't let him in the house. Then he began to stray farther and longer from home. After he was missing several days, I found him lying bloated by the roadside. I got the old blanket from my car, the one I put across the backseat for the two of them when we went places together, and spread it on the ground next to him. I tried to push his body onto it with my foot. Used to be I'd roll him back and forth on the floor like a hollow barrel—his jowls flopping open, his teeth bared in pleasure—but he was heavier than he'd been. Each disturbance I made to his body sent insects circling and redoubling their efforts.

A few cars passed. The sun began to beat on us. His smell rose from him in waves. I sat on the gravel. After a while, a pickup pulled to the side and a man got out. He took a few steps, then squatted on his heels and looked at us.

It's just going to get worse, he said.

I let him buy me a cup of coffee after. The cab of his truck was oily with labor. I smoked one of his cigarettes with the windows up and watched his hand on the gear shift, how the veins strained the skin—his fingers and knuckles marked with blue.

◆

I did not have a dog after that. I did not want one. I was busy and did not think about them much. But then I moved to a place where it seemed everyone had one, sometimes two or three. I went to where they kept them in great number and looked around, slowly walking the aisles that smelled of feces and bleach. I looked in their eyes and their eyes looked back, but it was hard to tell.

In the house next to me then lived a man and his three dogs, a type I hadn't seen before, very large—larger than the small man—with sharp, narrow snouts and glamorous long hair that framed their faces and gave them the appearance of strange, homely women, though when they barked they sounded like angry men. Whenever I am walking now and a man leans out of a slowing car to bark at me, I think of those dogs.

My neighbor's dogs were a constant trouble to him. I would see him driving his small car with all three of them inside—one in front and two in back—their noses out the windows, their hair streaming into the man's face as he hunched over the wheel. He could walk them only very early or very late when no one else was out—it seemed all he could do just to hang on while they dragged him down the street.

Unlike other men I've seen with a mean dog, my neighbor did not seem proud of them or proud of himself for raising them. Our houses almost touched. We kept our windows open all year. When he spoke to them it seemed he was speaking to me—his voice traveling clearly and firmly into my rooms, in a tone one might use with an employee or teenager.

I am not a dog, he said. You are a dog.

◆

Some nights a man would come to see me. I would open one of my doors but not the other and look at him through the screen before I unlocked it. The light above his head stuttered with moths and cast odd shadows. It was hard to tell where his bones ended. He never looked the same. I sometimes wondered whether I wasn't visited by a different, albeit similar man each night—and if that was the case, whether or not I minded.

There was a place where people gathered. That was where I met the man. I walked in one night after walking up and down the streets that led from where I lived. I'd walked to my car to get something from it. Then, after getting the thing, instead of returning to my house, I'd walked past it wishing I knew someone, some man, whose house I could walk to, upon whose door I could knock—a man I knew but not well, one I'd not seen in a while who would be surprised to find me on his step. But I did not know anyone, not even the man with the dogs next door, whose name I never learned, and whose face, when I try to think of it now, will not come to me.

As I walked away from my house, a cat—one without tail or ears—began to follow me. It was a cat I knew but had long since given up for dead. We passed uncurtained houses that released their odors like nocturnal flowers. We passed a tree hung with hollow bottles that moaned and made sounds of breaking when they touched. We passed a statue at the entrance to a church—a large wolf with pendulous teats, from which two naked baby boys suckled.

When we reached the place, the cat sat down at the entrance to wait. Inside, the lights were dim and there were pieces of wood nailed together for sitting on. People sat and stood in slumped and straight positions, and many clustered in the middle of the room. I pushed through them, though to what end I couldn't have said. Then a hand pressed my back and a voice near my ear said, *This is the way*. I liked the voice and I liked the hand, so we walked out the back together.

We walked under a large moon that lit the ground. The

path we followed was different from the one I'd come in on. This path was grass, with trees all around. The man walked with his face tilted up toward the sky. I walked looking from side to side. The dark growth twitched and crackled. I saw sets of eyes without bodies. I thought of fine teeth closing on my arm—the chaos of wire-stiff hair and hot, wet blood. I thought of what I would do. What the man would do.

I turned to the man. He opened his mouth and made a long sound. He made it again and again. While he made it, no other sound could be heard. It was a sound I'd heard before. It came from him in starts and stops in a rhythm that was not unfamiliar.

SALAD DAYS

Now we'd settled into something else—he and I.

Every other day, we got a coupon in the mail from the new casino downtown. They were offering ten dollars each to spend on slots and two free lunch buffets, so we went.

We arrived in the morning and helped ourselves to the complimentary rolls and coffee. Then we wandered around until a particular machine called to us. We sat down and played our ten dollars. And wouldn't you know—we won every time.

We'd cash out quickly and head to the buffet. They had a special fried shrimp dish on certain days, and a spectacular Jell-O salad we both enjoyed.

From there, we'd breeze out of the parking ramp with our validated ticket and drive directly to the golf course. A friend of his was the new manager there. If we came on a weekday before five, he'd forget to ring us up. He gave us keys to a cart and off we went.

We found sets of used clubs at a charity shop and kept them in the trunk. Mine came in a baby-blue bag of simulated leather. Each of the clubs was sheathed in a knitted blue-and-white sock with a pom-pom on top.

I got some athletic shoes, too. I had long-standing doubts about the category—their bulkiness and relationship to the size of my feet and the shape of my calves in general—and had never owned a pair.

You're right, he said when I tried them on in the sporting-goods store. They do look a little funny on you.

He was too competitive, and he drove the cart too fast. But for a while, I didn't mind the hustle. My game was improving. Our winnings were adding up on account of our low expenditure rate. I kept our tab in a little notebook.

When we returned the cart and tallied our scorecards with tiny pencils at the clubhouse canteen, his friend brought us rum-and-cokes in frosted glasses and bottomless bowls of popcorn and salted peanuts in the shell.

Then one night he went to use the bathroom before we left. I slid from my barstool and leaned over to tie my sneaker.

A hand landed on my ass. I stood up. His friend was there, grinning. He did not withdraw his hand.

I bet you like to fuck, the friend said.

On the way back to the apartment, we were all over the road. My husband was jerking the wheel. A fine mist coated the windshield, but he did not flip the switch to wipe it. He went to the bedroom right away and began to snore. I lay on the couch but did not sleep.

In the morning, we arrived late to the casino. The coffee and rolls had been cleared away, so we ordered from a waitress walking the floor. She returned with two tepid cupfuls and charged us four dollars. I made a mark in my notebook.

The bad coffee soured our empty stomachs. None of the slots looked like winners. The place was crowded with elderly types and chain-smokers. The machines trilled shrilly around us.

We gave up our divination routine at last and sat down at random machines on opposite sides of the room. Mine was called Aces Wild. I plunked down the money and yanked the arm. I pulled dud after dud. Then my ten dollars was gone.

I found him slouched across a vinyl banquette. He shook his head.

At the buffet, the offerings were unrecognizable. We questioned the hostess, who told us a new chef had been hired.

What about the special shrimp? we said. And the Jell-O salad?

Have you tried the crawfish étouffée? she said.

Because we'd forgotten to stamp our parking ticket, we paid the smug cashier eight dollars to release us. I made another notation.

At the golf course, the friend was nowhere to be seen. A teenager greeted us at the clubhouse window. That'll be eighteen dollars, she said.

I want to play, he said, turning toward me.

So I reached into my billfold, plucked a crisp twenty, and handed it over.

I'd never seen him play so poorly. I was beating him on every hole. He hit into the scrub every time. He lost ball after ball. He cursed. He stood rigidly, hands on his hips, shaking his head in disgust. He spit on the grass and grunted.

As we drove toward the last hole, it began to rain. The grass slickened. He took us downhill—fast.

Then he made a sharp, unexpected turn—and I flew. I landed on my back several yards away.

He braked abruptly, then looked back at me. The party on the neighboring hole stopped their game.

Get up, he said.

A man from the other party waved. Everything okay? he called.

Get up, he said. People are looking.

The rain was falling lightly on my face. The grass was cool beneath me.

Get up, goddamn it, he said. He got out of the cart and walked toward me.

And then—like some kind of miracle—someone shouted, *Fore!* and a neon-green ball materialized. It struck him on the side of the head. He made a sound like a cushion deflating. He fell to the ground.

The rain continued to fall. Way up above us, the clouds—tired of the same old thing—were rapidly changing their patterns.

LIVE A LITTLE

We're getting fat, I said. We need to go on a diet.

Not me, he said. I'm the perfect weight. I haven't got a pound to lose.

We'll see, I said.

In the kitchen, my cupboards were a mess. I kept buying cookware. I had duplicates of everything—quart pan, stockpot, deep fryer, double boiler. It had gotten so crowded in there I'd stopped cooking altogether. Instead, we ordered takeout and turned on the food channel. There was a show about baking we particularly enjoyed.

I exerted myself for an hour and emerged with the steam basket and the lidded pot it fit into. I'd also found the air popper, the blender, the strainer, and the big wooden salad bowl with the matching tongs we'd gotten as a wedding gift. The finish on the wood was tacky—like the range top after a bacon fry.

I washed everything in the sink and arranged it on a towel on the counter to dry. On the bookshelf, I found *Staying Slim the Scandinavian Way*, which I'd bought for its photographs of the Swedish author—a young model at the time of publication. In one photo, she sat at a dinette—barefoot, laughing, her long, tan legs crossed at the thigh—bringing a small chunk of melon to her mouth. In another, dressed in a thick white sweater, she cupped a mug tenderly.

According to the Swede, breakfast was black coffee with fruit. Lunch was a scoop of cottage cheese stuffed into a tomato. For dinner, there was a broth you made by dissolving a single cube of bouillon in boiling water.

I got into the car and drove to the grocery store. I pulled a cart from the queue and rolled it toward the produce aisle.

Mr. Lipincott, the produce manager, was there, stacking lemons.

Mr. Lipincott, I said—I need your help.

Oh? he said. He held the last lemon in his hand. He was attempting to place it, but it was a wobbler.

I need tomatoes, I said. A lot of them.

He turned to where the tomatoes were arrayed in a wide swath upon a tilted table.

Here are some very good ones, he said. They've just come in. Very juicy.

I'm sure they are, I said. They look wonderful. My problem is your price.

Three dollars a pound is a standard tomato price. Ask anyone, he said.

That's news to me, I said. They're about the easiest thing in the world to grow.

I wouldn't know, he said.

Here's another thing, I said. How do you look your neighbors in the face when you're charging them a dollar each for these pears?

Those are excellent pears, ma'am, he said. They're a very special variety. They get flown here on an airplane. Each one gets put in a little padded sleeve to protect it during shipment.

I had a pear tree once, and the thing was a nuisance, I said. It made a huge mess. Maybe you should've come over to my yard with your little sleeves and picked them up for me.

Is there something in particular you need tomatoes and pears for? he asked. Are you following a recipe?

My husband and I are getting fat, I said.

When I got home, my husband was watching a program about a South American drug cartel. He had the volume all the way up.

Turn that down, I said. I'm trying to concentrate.

I put the kettle on the burner and set the knob to high. I plucked two foil-wrapped cubes from the jar. I unwrapped them and plopped them in.

When it was ready, I brought the mugs into the living room with me. I handed him one and sat down on the edge of an ottoman.

What's this? he asked.

Dinner, I said.

Sure it is, he said.

It's Scandinavian, I said. Why don't you live a little? For once?

On the screen, a dark-haired man in a three-piece suit stepped out of a flashy car. He wore a thick gold chain around his neck, dark sunglasses. He carried a large leather briefcase.

The man looked to the left and right. He crossed a busy street quickly, then disappeared into a crowd shopping at an open-air market. In the end, we learned, he was never caught.

DESIGN FOR A CARPET

It must fit in the spot allotted for it—no larger, no smaller. It must give pleasure to a naked foot, yet not be so thick as to trip us. The corners must not flip up at the slightest provocation. It must lay smooth and flat—undisturbed by our trodding.

Its pleasing colors must be arranged in a pleasing way. Our eyes must receive a little thrill whenever they pass over it—morning and evening—day after day—year after year.

The dog must like to recline there. The dog's deposit of hair must rise readily to the vacuum's suck—but the color and pattern of the carpet must also disguise the hair so that if no vacuuming occurs, the carpet looks presentable nonetheless.

When we wash it, it must not bleed.

When we dry it, it must not stubbornly stay wet.

When we hang it over the railing to beat, it must not resist.

We do not wish to have to repair it, but if we must, the repair must be an easy one that requires no particular skill or knowledge.

We must not disagree about the carpet. One of us must not suddenly desire a new carpet while the other still enjoys the original. The carpet must not create discordance of any kind in the house.

There must never be a time when we look at the carpet and are left cold, or feel regret, or wish we had made a different choice. We must always feel that, of all the carpets available to us, we have selected the very best one.

If we do tire of the carpet, we must be able to rid ourselves of it easily, casually, as one tosses a paper cup. We must never look at the bare floor, or the new carpet, and wonder what was so wrong with the old one, and who walked on it now.

THE WINE MANAGER AND I

The wine manager and I picnicked endlessly. He organized it all in a large basket manufactured expressly for the purpose, with special slots for the cutlery and a long, tubular compartment to snug the bottle. He selected a different vintage for every meal and carefully chose the foods to best enhance its flavor.

He was slightly older than I, with thin white hair and a body that might not be disagreeable. I had been styling my hair suggestively for years. These days, I wore it in the traditional crop of the elderly. Before that, I'd spun it 'round and 'round like a silken cone—wrapped in an airy scarf.

Here at last was the calm life. On his checkered blanket, spread across the grass of some park or other, we would sit until the large plants around us began to cast man-shaped shadows.

Try this, he said. What he offered was refreshing—something dry, cold, deeply pink, lightly bitter—slightly spitting. It crackled in my ear like a big black fly can.

TA-DA!

A child was talking, or trying to, on the other side of the garden fence, yet the child did not sound like a child. This must be a man, I thought—a sad, tired, sloppy drunk of a certain age, attempting to express his disappointment with life.

Buh buh buh buh, said the child.

I passed a man a little later on a tall ladder near a robust tree and there came a sudden noise from him—a rough heave-and-ho, a rhythmic panting, huffing. What this man was doing was making loud sexual sounds. But when I looked up, I saw that the man held a saw, and that the sexual sounds were the sounds of the saw's blade cutting the wet orange flesh of the tree. As I walked away, the noise changed again— this time becoming the comical splutter of several forceful farts.

On my way back down the street, the dusk was darkening the houses and shrubs from the ground up, like dye climbing a cloth. This was the shaded side of the hill and on a bright day would be ten degrees cooler than the sunny side.

Below me, in a yard that sloped steeply into a deep gulch, I heard the pronounced rustle of disturbed underbrush, and I saw that a large shrub was shaking dramatically. I was reminded of the dream I have from time to time, wherein a German shepherd tears off an arm of mine. Then I thought of the old tale of some bush that had once shuddered with the spirit of the Lord—or had it burned?

Slowly, from the shrub's thick, dark leaves, a bare arm emerged. Then a denim-clad leg struggled forth, attached to a foot housed in a white athletic shoe. It was clear by now that a difficult birth was under way.

I've always been a sucker for origin stories, so I held my breath and waited to see how this one might begin.

YET YOU TURN TO THE MAN

The cat was dying too slow. The vet could end it but the vet was thirty miles away and the cat hated the car.

I called the vet. Could I get it—what he used? Could I pick it up and bring it home and do it to her—by syringe or pill or however one did?

Can't let you have it, said the vet. He told me the drug he used was the same drug a person will drop in a date's drink in order to rape the date later. I could go to jail, he said.

Well, I don't plan on raping anyone, I said.

The vet said, Does your husband own a gun?

He did. At the end, he kept it on the bed next to him when we had sex. But now he was gone, and so was the gun.

I hung up the phone and went to the garage. There were tools—loppers, rakes, hammers, screwdrivers, saws. I picked up the rusted shovel and went to where the cat lay on her side in the grass, panting.

She was slightly slovenly, a little stupid. She'd been a bad mother. But she purred when you touched her and she had a pretty face. Now she trembled. Her fine fur was knotted in large, hard clumps. Every few minutes, one leg shot straight out, and the toes of the foot clutched at the air.

I lifted the shovel above my head and held it there. I pictured the person who could do this—someone stronger than I was. This person would hit the cat's head—hard—with the flat back of the shovel. If a second hit was needed, or a third, fourth, fifth, this person—let's be clear, this man—would ignore the blood. If the cat screamed or squirmed, the man would take no notice. He would calmly finish his task.

He is a practical man. He'd clean the shovel of blood with the dirt he'd dig to make a hole to put the dead cat in. If you cried for the cat, he'd tell you to stop being a dumb cunt.

The man's presence means a plowed drive, a car that starts, a cord of firewood, a freezer full of dismembered deer. At night, there is a feeling some might call safety, yet you turn to the man even when it is the man of whom you are afraid.

But now he's headed up where the work is rough— splitting rocks, cutting trees, gutting fish. With any luck, the work will break the man like I can snap a cooked chicken bone with one hand.

VAGRANTS

When we had no money we'd get in our car, and if it started and had gas enough, we'd drive until we came to streets unlike the one we lived on, where we'd creep along and gawk at the splendid order of affluence. We rolled the windows down to lean like dogs into the open air—so fresh there. We waved at all who passed. The wealthy are naturally suspicious and seldom waved back, but we didn't grudge them so long as we were gazing ourselves full on their bounty.

I'd call out the houses that suited me, but he often found my choices too provincial. If my mood was raw, I'd take offense, then quarrel with whatever else he said or sink into a silent sulk. In this way, I believe the experience closely resembled house shopping in earnest, though I can't say for certain, as I've never had more than the rent that comes due so often—how quickly a month passes, it never fails to startle.

But sometimes we agreed. On that rare occasion, we'd pull to the curb to admire our decision—a sound investment with a great deal of potential. The landscaping, for instance, left much to be desired, but that we could work on together. Digging holes and filling them—that was something we could do.

As we sat looking from the curb, the interior of the house we'd chosen would take shape in our heads.

Mine would be empty—stripped to the subfloor—with sunlight falling unimpeded through bare, blindless windows. What I craved was an echo.

But his? How long were his halls, how wide his rooms? What was the feel of his banister beneath a sliding hand?

If the weather was right, our moods expansive, we would come by cautious conversation to conclude that two houses might be best. That way, if we tired of one, we might leave it a while. The thought of that, the space of it, would fill our small car. If we tired of one. Another.

Oh, but the work—it could drag on for years! Mornings, we'd attempt toast amongst flaked paint—every surface dusted with the fine white powder of demolition. We'd endure the chaos of shadeless table lamps, tarped furniture, functionless plumbing, plastic forks. Clutching some foam box of gluey takeout, we'd huddle the television set like tramps at a barrel fire—vagrants as ever.

We lived like peasants in our one-room apartment, stepping over each other to get to the toilet. Left for days on the line in the sun, our grimed sheets never whitened. In the refrigerator were some turnips, in the cupboard a handful of rice. You can think of it as a game if you like—the sort enjoyed by hobbyists who assemble to reenact great battles in which many lives were lost and limbs, too, sawn from their owners awake.

There was a small windfall once, but we spent it on whiskey and purple-skinned nectarines and steaks in soft sacks of blue blood and some pretty plates for eating on that since have broken—all. I made a halting half-moon ridge of them in our patch of dirt—for what purpose? None but to remember how we ate once—no longer.

When we returned at last to the sun-dappled street, the tidy curb, our car seemed shabbier, and the lawns beyond looked remote and ridiculously green.

He was usually the one to drive. I could tell by the way he shifted the car into gear that we were done for the day. He'd steer us through light and shade—away. His tolerance for looking at the unattainable was so much lower than mine, which felt boundless, untested. It was the only thing I wanted to see.

NOW THIS

I'd already washed smoke from my hair for the day—now this. The one who usually roasted the pig was sick, so the rest of us had to guess how. We lit enough charcoal to cook four. The poor blackened body, eyeless, scorched in its fat until dark. We bore it to the woods on a busted raft. The crisp carbon skin flaked like mica. We were an hour digging, then an hour covering the hissing corpse with wet, heavy dirt. When we got back, sooty and sore, we ate cold rolls spread with catsup. When that wasn't enough, we gulped relish from the jar. When that wasn't enough, each of us turned to our own hands, taking pleasure in the unexpected flavor we found there—smoky, salty, not unlike things we'd tasted before.

DEAR MARY

By now you must think me infirm or dead. I was both for a time. But I want to tell you now that I am alive. I want you to know it, so that you'll think better of me when you think of me, if you think of me.

In the beginning it was hard. My God. You can imagine. I'm not asking for sympathy. We all of us have our lot.

Things were lost. We pitched them over. Our salt jar, our heavy table. Our spoons, our lamps, our rugs and other comforts.

When I started digging in the dirt I found a hole, descending. And another. I found any number of omens, none of them good, but I kept at it.

There was a storm with no rain. It shook us and turned everything over. It made the night darker. I looked out to the tallest tree and it seemed to me a tall, slim woman with a head of hair. The abundance of her hair made a sound like waves crashing. All night. All night. The poor woman was tossed and disheveled so roughly.

The neighbor's house burned. It started with a small flame in one corner, licking out like some little cat's tongue. The men—I suppose it could be said they tried. They scrambled across the roof with their limp streams. You would've laughed, too. The flames were in an uproar. Walking past at night, I hold my breath. The sky, which is so big and hard here, it comes right through the top. It comes through the windows from the inside out.

My clothes all need mending, but I am mending them as we speak. My shabbiness—it could never reach you, far apart as we are now.

Dear Mary, I was ill. I had a fever. Of the brain. A general hollowing-out. A weakening and a withering. A failure to thrive. A most deadly consumption. I soaked the counterpane. Night after night. Night after night. It went on this way.

Don't ask me how it ended. I couldn't tell you. There was no elixir. No poultice. It was really very mysterious. I couldn't say any more than that. It was simple. I would not call it miraculous.

THE OLD MILL

J lives at the top of French Hill Road and I live at the bottom. When he comes for me I can hear him coming. If I'm holding a cup of coffee when he gets in his car and starts it, my coffee cup will shudder in my hand. But when that happens I need only set it down, the cup, onto a table or near the sink. I put on my jacket and put my hands in the pockets.

One of us asks the other, You hungry or anything? and the other says, No.

J complains about my makeup on his face, but I keep wearing it. Without it I look too much like myself.

When it's warm we party in a field, a ring of cars and trucks around a fire, and when it's cold we party in Stu's basement because no one else has a basement and Stu's dad doesn't give a fuck.

This your girl? Stu's dad asks J, jerking his thumb. Later

I hear Stu's dad tell Stu that I look like a nice normal dick-loving girl.

When we don't feel like the field or Stu's basement, we party on the river by the old mill. We have to walk through the woods and down a steep hill to get there. No one likes the old mill anymore because it's slippery getting down and it's cold and once Stu fell in and got sucked under by the water. But J and I still like it, and we go there together.

Stu has an old dog, Old Bruno. Stu likes to smoke a joint and blow the smoke into Old Bruno's face. The dog's face used to be brown but now it's white. He doesn't have much hair left on his tail, so when it wags it's a whip. Stu hates getting whipped, and starts yelling and shoving the dog until the tail is tucked away and still.

I fucking hate Stu, that motherfucker.

Tonight J and I are going to the old mill. At the Kum & Go, we get a bottle of champagne and some cigarettes. Christy is working the register. She likes J, and keeps looking at him.

For a while Stu was calling me in the middle of the night, leaving four or five messages in a row. I never picked up. He'd talk about when we were little kids together. I'd wake up and hear him on the machine and think he was in the house, in my room.

The old mill used to be dark red, but now it's sprayed with vulgar stuff in bright colors. People broke the windows with rocks. The wheel fell apart a long time ago, busted into pieces and drifted downriver.

Stu brings one of his dad's guns to the field and sets up

cans on rocks to shoot at. He drains his beers fast because he needs the cans. It gets dark, and he comes over to the fire. He wants to show me the gun, but I don't want to look at it. I keep shaking and turning my head until he puts it against my cheek. Then I don't move at all.

J and I are going away. I put my favorite things in a suitcase. At the top of French Hill Road, I hear an engine revving.

The bottom of the mill stretches right into the river, and the water shoves up against it hard, like it's trying to tear it apart. I guess eventually it will.

We drive until dark, stopping only for pops and to piss by the side of the road. It feels like we're being chased, but we don't say anything. We turn the radio up. We're just having fun, doing something different.

At the motel, they give us a bunch of coupons. $1 Towards any beverage at our Twilight Bar & Lounge (Live Band Karaoke Fridays), $1 Towards any entree at the Family Restaurant OR Grill-Your-Own Texas Steakhouse. House Specialties: Iron Rich Baby Beef Liver. Roast Young Tom Turkey. Roast Loin of Pork. Country Style Veal Cutlet. Freshly Made Chopped Steak. Stuffed Flounder.

I don't remember meeting J. It's like he was always there, but suddenly got brighter—like when you stare at the ground an hour before you see your dropped earring and wonder how you could've missed it.

We pull our curtains tight and double-lock the door and sit on the bed, passing our little bottle. Just outside our room, late, a man's voice comes low and sad—Bill. Bill. Hey, Bill. He gets louder—Bill. Hey, BILL. Then he shouts—HEY, WHAT'RE YOU CRYING FOR, BILL? WHY DON'T YOU STOP CRYING? STOP CRYING, YOU FUCKING FAGGOT, AND LET ME IN.

J falls asleep but I can't. Channel 1: A Texas Ranger protects five college cheerleaders. Channel 16: A private investigator who is a vampire. Channel 24: A dorky teen attends a high school for superheroes. Channel 38: A grungy criminal and a teen queen magically switch bodies. Channel 40: A couple is stranded at a hotel. Channel 56: A tycoon offers a cash-strapped couple $1 million. Channel 59: Tale of racial prejudice between Indians and whites. Channel 60: Rendered obsolete, a hardened soldier is abandoned.

In the morning we will get in the car and drive. Maybe we will stop and drink coffee or eat a donut. We'll stay in another place like this. The scenery will not be much different. But the day after that, and the day after that for sure, I think things will start to change.

The river coming over the big rocks at the old mill is loud—so loud! You can't hear anything else. You don't need to talk. J and I just look at each other. That's it.

Sometimes I'd turn around like someone was sneaking up behind me. I'd stare into the woods and the woods would stare back. When I looked too long at the fast black water, it tried to pull me in. But I'll miss that place, and I hope I never see it again.

FABLE

The girl's mother sent her to the store for meat, but the girl, when she arrived, could not remember which cut was requested, or even which animal. She stood with a hand resting lightly on the cool glass of the case until the butcher—a bachelor handsome to some but repulsive to others—approached, wiping his hands of the blood that accompanied his trade.

What does the young lady require? he asked, looking at each part of her with his professional's eye.

The girl was among those who found the butcher repulsive, so she turned to leave, suppressing the rise of a gag.

Perhaps, he called, if nothing here will suit, she would like to see something else—out back?

The girl's curiosity often led her into troublesome situations, but she considered it part of the pact her soul had made in order to gain entrance to the world, and did not worry much over what befell her. Behind the butcher's shop was a little dirt yard where a dog was tied, surrounded by many gnawed bones. Sitting on a stump of wood was a large iron skillet.

I made that, he said. Lift it, he said.

But the girl could not lift it, and she wrinkled her face in displeasure. What good is a skillet you can't lift? she said.

The butcher frowned. He gripped the handle and swung it easily, carelessly. He thought of swinging it against the girl's head but knew the timing was not right.

The girl walked to where the dog was tied and squatted beside it. What a pair you make, said the butcher. And indeed the picture gave him a great deal of pleasure. It rippled up and down his arms and legs, erecting the many dark hairs to be found there. To get a better look, he strode to where the girl was and gripped her by the back of the neck. He lifted her easily, carelessly.

The girl limped home carrying a packet of liver, but by the time she arrived, her mother was gone. It was just as well, she thought—her mother hated liver.

The girl waited many days, but her mother did not return.

She sat in a dry tub upstairs, eating crackers and thinking. Occasionally she stood to peer from the high, narrow window into the yard below, but the grass and other plants lay drab and useless as ever.

She concluded that her mother must finally have found the man she'd been seeking since the departure of the girl's father on the eve of her birth. She knew her mother to be a kind woman, but one ultimately dominated by the demands of her sex, which—as she aged—became increasingly totalitarian.

◆

News of the girl's marriage to the butcher was received without surprise or comment by the people of the town. But after she'd been married a month, the girl—who really was still a girl—saw that what she'd endeavored to understand was not so complex. It wouldn't do. She rose in the night to roam the woods that edged the town, and there learned many interesting things. The sky was cold and distant and hard, but no matter—she obscured it with her smoke.

Mornings before work, the butcher blackened iron and hammered it into shape on his hobbyist's anvil. He blackened the girl, too, but she was less malleable than he'd hoped, so he kept her out back with the dog while he sawed bones and clasped hands in his immaculate shop, his white teeth testimony enough for any who might ask.

The dog was an old gray-faced bitch. She was too old to bear pups, but she cared for the girl as best she was able. When the girl was cold, she warmed her, and when the girl was hurt, she licked the wound until it healed. But when the girl died, there was nothing to be done—and the dog sank into a silent dream.

An abundance of flowers surrounded the girl at her funeral,

an event well attended by the people of the town. She did not look quite dead, which eased the proceedings.

To everyone's astonishment, a handsome stranger was soon recognized—the girl's father, returned at last. How had he come to be there on that particular day? How far had he traveled? Where had he been and what had he seen these many years? The father stood at the center of the crowd, shaking hands, his smile wide and benign.

The girl's father spent what remained of the day with the butcher, who prepared a hearty meal of his choicest cuts. The two men took a quick liking to each other. As they ate, the father said, Tell me, butcher—what was she like?

The butcher—saddened suddenly by the absence of the girl—could think of nothing to say. She was always hungry, he pronounced at last, and she enjoyed eating whatever was placed in front of her.

When they finished, they stepped outside to admire the slow decline of the sun. They walked in a leisurely fashion, arriving finally at a little pond beloved for its middling beauty. Along its banks lay heaps of small, smooth stones, which they kneeled on to paw through. Handled properly, a good stone would jig happily, prettily across the surface until exhausted. As the men understood it, the trick was to hold the thing lightly—tenderly—and then, with a swift jerk, send it spinning.

After they'd been at it a while with some success, they paused to observe a pair of figures a little farther down the shore.

Well, would you look at that, said the father, shading his eyes for a better view.

It was the butcher's old bitch—awake now, and mounted on the hindquarters of a young rascal about town, an impregnator par excellence. She gripped his neck with her teeth. Though he cried and struggled, she took her pleasure with the strength of one suddenly possessed by some fresh and vigorous spirit.

MASTER FRAMER

He said he'd studied under an old master of the trade. He was with the old master until the master died. From the master, he learned all there was to know.

They felt lucky to hire him. They had a stack of lithographic prints—playful, pandering Parisian street scenes—which they intended to sell for tidy sums at a tony local street fair. The master framer began work at once, with an industry they admired from their office, where they looked up from paperwork to nod in approbation.

Then one day he came in gray, disheveled, wearing what he'd worn the day before. They asked what the matter was. His wife, he said. She'd changed the locks and put his things on the lawn. He'd put the things in his car and driven to the parking lot of a large discount store, where he spent the night.

He set his shoes outside the car while he slept, and when he woke, they were gone.

They saw that instead of sneakers, he wore stiff leather wingtips, which gave him a professional air despite his rumpled hair and clothing. They suggested he sleep on the sofa in the workshop until he got himself sorted.

Weeks passed. When they unlocked the workshop in the morning, the master framer snored open-mouthed on the sofa in his undershorts, often with an erection in plain view. The oily brine of his unbathed body—soured by the odor of discount cologne—grimed the beige upholstery.

After the master framer stepped out for lunch one afternoon, whistling a tune and wishing them well, they approached his workstation with caution. He always looked busy, so they didn't worry. But today they picked a finished frame from his stack and held it beneath the special lamp they'd purchased for this purpose.

Ah, see—very nice! said one.

What is that? said the other.

Beneath the glass, on the white mat board, was a smear of peanut butter, stuck with cracker crumbs—oozing dark oil.

Disgusting! said one.

A fluke, said the other.

But they found some offensive object encased in each of the frames in the master's stack: a green crust of nasal mucus—multiple kinky hairs—a crushed potato chip—a scattering of dandruff—even some drops of brown blood.

Too, the corners of the frames were crooked. The screws—sent in sideways, hard—split the wood. Glue oozed in rigid, sculptural drips. Not one was usable. They cried and exchanged bitter words of blame.

When the master framer returned from lunch, his box of things sat soggily on the sidewalk and his key would not unbolt the lock. No one answered when he knocked. He put his ear to the door. He looked up and down the street. A little white dog lifted its leg on his box. He gave chase, but the dog danced easily out of reach. Winded, the master framer heaved the box into his car and drove away.

He never saw them again—his employers—but he did see one of their prints hanging in a bathroom in the house of a wealthy woman who hired him for odd jobs some years later. She needed her trees trimmed and her leaves blown and the crap of her dog scooped from the lawn, where she liked to walk barefoot after a pedicure.

When he'd performed these services tolerably well for a few weeks, she offered him the modest guest quarters above her garage. She liked the master framer—liked him even better when he told her he'd framed the print in her bathroom, which she prized.

What a marvelous coincidence, she said. What fine work. What a man of many talents you are.

THE RESCUED MAN

They're good dogs, I said, as the pups crapped where they stood, stepped in it, then tumbled toward him.

He held each one and looked into its eyes. He took it up by the legs, the throat, the snout. He tugged on the tail and ears. He laid it on its back to see what it would do. He said he was looking for the one that wouldn't do anything. That was the dog, he said, you could really teach. He chose the runt of the litter, the one I called Little Jim.

He's a sweet one, Little Jim, I said, while I waited for the man to shuck from his rubber-banded bill roll.

You're a sweet one, the man said. He stepped closer with the money. Then, instead of handing it to me, he grabbed my hair and twisted it. His other hand darted around my body, into its pockets, like he was searching for some small item I'd hidden. But then he let go and stepped back. He breathed heavily and wiped his mouth. He picked up the pup from where it sat. He got into his truck and drove away with Little Jim lying like a potato in the trough of his lap.

A few years later, I heard about how this same man tied his leg to a concrete block and walked into the river. A fisherman motored over to where the man had slipped under, and with hooks and nets hauled him out of the water and onto the deck of the boat, but the man resisted. Violence became necessary, said the fisherman. To save the man, he beat him on the head.

The rescued man was taken to a place for cases like his and never heard from again. Out-of-town relations arrived to disperse his holdings. They affixed a price tag to every item in his house, then opened the doors on a Saturday morning. The proceeds would pay, in perpetuity, the people who now protected the man from his unnatural intentions.

Winona Goldstone parked her truck out front to sell loose beef sandwiches and pie slices. As usual, she cut her coffee with decaf, so you had to buy two for the jolt of one. Everyone was there—Mort, Pinkie, Gigi, Hep, Jeff, Hal, Winterbottom, and Arliss—even Bob Snatchko showed up.

At one end of the house was a large room set up like an artist's studio. There was an easel with an unfinished canvas propped up on it and a little table strewn with bottles and tubes of paint and thinner. The walls were densely hung. I paused to inspect some awkward landscapes done in sulky blues and grays.

Then, in a corner on a stool, I saw it—the head of the rescued man himself. It was made of rough pink clay that looked raw, porous—like anything dripped or poured on it would be sucked deep into the man's head. His lips curled in bitter, enduring disappointment.

Bob Snatchko held a painting of yellow flowers in dirty snow. Looks like we had a genius on our hands, he said. What a tragedy! Are these things worth more now that he's a confirmed nut job?

Some pie on your chin, Bob, I said.

When I got to the kitchen, there he was—Little Jim! The dog—with the distinctive white star of fur on his brisket—stood as still and regal as the dog statues you see in the yards of people who put on airs.

A woman stepped out of the pantry holding a can of chunky noodle soup. That is the most well-trained animal on the planet, she said. Try him if you don't believe me. Shake! she shouted.

The dog glanced at the woman, for whom he seemed to have no particular affinity. Yet he raised one leg and let it hang until I grasped it.

See? said the woman. Now watch this. Lie down!

The dog eased himself gingerly, grudgingly to the floor.

Roll over!

The dog rolled over quickly, then jumped up into a rigid, embarrassed posture.

Speak!

The dog barked once, twice. His voice was mournful. He resumed his original position, sitting quietly, watching the people who came and went through the front door.

Amazing, isn't it, said the woman.

◆

In one hand I held his leash, and in the crook of my other arm, I cradled the man's head. Around us, people hustled to their cars with what they'd bought.

When we got home, I took him to a small clearing. I unbolted his leash and removed his collar. Then, utilizing a set of techniques I'd devised, I untrained him. Little Jim struggled and cried. He was confused. At last he understood. When we returned to the house, he zigged and zagged with a buoyant tail. He stopped to flop and roll on his back in the dirt. He flushed some squirrels from a bush and bounded off in a howl.

Inside, I got us some cool water and slices of roast. The head of the rescued man sat on the sill of the picture window that overlooked the pond. The green reflection of the water made the man look like he might be imminently, violently sick.

I picked up the man's head. It was smaller than life— I could hold it in one hand. I studied it, then placed it back on the sill. There it sat, and there it continues to sit—another vulnerable relic collecting dust.

LEMONS

My lemons are coming along fat but misshapen, some better than others, and some have fallen already to the ground. I grate their skins, and when they are bald and soft and white, slice and squeeze them limp.

I let her in and touch her shoulders. She has brought nothing with her.

The thing I've made is resting. It has a powder I don't like to disturb, but I cut it apart and set it between us. She does not touch her fork but continues to talk.

I lift a portion onto her plate. She severs a wedge and brings it to her mouth. She eats slowly, with sober ownership. The interior crumbles and the morning has begun to disappear. By night it will be gone.

I get the pitcher and pour out two sour glasses. I look at

the shrubs as I drink. My glass drips down my front. The spots widen across the ridges and valleys of cloth.

When she leaves I will give her the rest of it, pressed in plastic. I'll close the door on her back. I will wash my glass and hers, shake the cloth in the lawn, dump the skins in the can. As I move from room to room, fresh ones will start to come. They will tumble down one after another. They will knock me on the head and roll across the floor, across rooms, out into the street, and farther, even, than that.

THE POKER

I smeared my daughter's body with zinc cream and sat her—
a bonneted, white-frosted bun—on the bench next to me.
My own skin I oiled with a product that promised to brown it.

When the game was done and the requisite slapping of
hands and asses complete, the players emerged with dripping
cans of icy beer. My husband took his time. The big russet-
haired player, on the other hand—let's call him Struther—
was first to come out. He'd brush past his admirers—the
dependable cluster—and head straight for us.

Here they are, he'd say. What can I get for my girls—some
pop? A candy bar? Your wish is Uncle Struther's command!

He was always asking to hold my daughter, and when my
arms got tired or I wanted to do something else with them
for a few minutes, I let him. But once, while I queued at the
snack shack, I looked back and there was something wrong

about his hand—how it cupped her bottom, how it probed. Across one huge, ropy arm, her little legs splayed wide. I threw my cigarette to the ground. I flew. I grabbed and lifted, but he held on. My daughter started to cry.

No need to be greedy, Struther said.

But it was a season of pleasure and we mostly enjoyed it—my daughter, my husband, and I. We slept on the screened porch and ate fruit from roadside stands. We stopped at street carnivals to try our luck. My husband was luckier than most—he got our girl a big stuffed horse. We sat with her between us in a giant teacup that spun slowly on its saucer.

Then, after the last game of the year, on a night my husband was out of town, the doorbell rang. Struther was on the stoop. Could he take my daughter for an ice cream?

She's sick, I said. From the window I watched him walk back to his truck. He started it but sat in the cab a long, loud time before leaving. From the tailpipe came a thin blue smoke I could still smell later, when I sat in the bath.

At work the next day, I picked up the phone. Mr. Johnson's office, I said, How can I help you?

You can help me with my huge cock, said the caller.

Struther? I said. Is that you?

No, he said, and hung up.

◆

Then I was pregnant again.

Before I started to show, Mr. Johnson asked: Can I use

your daughter? She'd sit on Santa's lap ten minutes while a camera rolled. The commercial would be good for business, he said—and my bonus.

My daughter was lifted, tickled, fluffed. They painted her face. A man carried her across the set like a china vase and placed her on the broad velvet thigh of the man impersonating the fiction I'd recently sketched for her in vague strokes.

He comes into our house at night when we're asleep, I'd said.

My daughter's large, dark eyes took in the room. They turned to the face of the man who held her. Beneath his curly white beard, he was a haggard, bloated youth.

Okay, honey, look pretty, Mr. Johnson said, which was what he always said. I thought of my daughter on a screen, late at night, in a lonely den.

I strode across the set, plucked her from the man's lap, and walked out. In the bathroom, I wiped her face with wet towels. On the way home, I stopped at a lake. We sat on the grass. Brazen ducks approached but departed abruptly when they saw we had nothing to give them.

On Monday, Mr. Johnson called me to his office. I waited ten minutes for him to emerge from his private bathroom. At last the flush resounded and he came out, fastening himself. He sat at his desk and leaned back.

I had two things to do today, he said. Take a shit and fire you.

◆

At home, I tried crafts. I melted wax in a pan and poured it into molds I'd cut from milk cartons. But the cartons split and the wax flowed quickly into the sink and down the drain, where it promptly hardened. It took the grim plumber six hours to scrape it out.

Lady, he said when he left, stick to sewing, okay?

I bought a stack of cookbooks and attempted various bakes and dinners. One night, chopping onions, I cut my hand to the bone—I saw it, white, swimming in the brimming gash. In a damp, tingling suit of skin, I slid to the floor. Later—how much?—my husband shook me awake and drove me to the hospital.

Ouch, I said to the nurse who stitched me.

That hurts? she said.

Yes, I said.

That doesn't hurt, she said.

♦

My doctor asked: did I want a natural or an unnatural birth?

I need something for the pain, I told the old doctor. I was his last delivery before retirement.

I'm so tired of all you women, he said.

When it was over, I had another daughter. It was summer and I was high. They'd cut me, anus to vagina—no matter. I lay in bed with my girls. The smell of flowers came in. We slept.

I had a dream. On the porch, with my foot, I rocked the

baby in her bassinet. Then, with its cruel mouth, a large, muscular dog picked her up like she was a bone. It ran. I chased—too slow. The dog stopped to shake its toy. The baby screamed.

I'll get you some pills if you want, my husband said.

Flowers shriveled and our shocked lawn blanched beige. I drowsed through the house, bumping walls and tables. There was a sense of the earth in a fever. There was a question of when she'd boil over.

I gave birth again—this time to the clotted, rotted wad of gauze the old doctor'd stuffed me with to stop my blood.

I got him on the phone. I think you forgot something, I said.

You survived, didn't you? he said.

◆

Then, on the porch, on a day suspended by insect drone, we held our hands above our heads and turned them as though the breeze might be twisted on like a faucet. The older girl laughed and the younger one burped and bubbled at the mouth.

In a dark corner of the yard, something shifted. The drone stopped short—clamped tight.

Shadow became shape. The shape moved in our direction. It flickered like a flame. It wobbled, watery. It picked up speed. Then—fully formed—it advanced on us like a vision of God, gnashing his great white teeth.

Flesh of my flesh—I hauled them into the house. From the rack of fireplace tools, I picked up the poker. I went back out and shut the door firmly behind me.

All of this is just to say I have seen mine enemy upon the earth—and I smote him.

ACKNOWLEDGMENTS

These stories first appeared, some in a slightly different form, in *American Short Fiction*: "The Hungry Valley"; in *Caketrain*: "The Baby," "Coolly, Bluely," "Dear Mary," "Lemons," "Power Tools"; in *Egress*: "Dear Sirs," "Florida Is for Lovers," "Small Pink Female"; in *Everyday Genius*: "Victorian Wedding Portrait"; in *Fence*: "The Dominant Animal"; in *Gigantic*: "Master Framer"; in *Granta*: "The Poker"; in *The Iowa Review* (winner of the 2010 Fiction Prize): "The Old Mill"; in *Juked*: "Vagrants"; in *New York Tyrant*: "Design for a Carpet"; in *NOON*: "Bait-and-Switch," "Beef Hearts Trimmed of Fat, Braised," "BJ," "The Candidate," "Derland," "The First Whiffs of Spring," "Happy Wife, Happy Life," "Line," "Live a Little," "Mother's Teeth," "Playhouse," "Please," "The Rescued Man," "Salad Days," "Ta-Da!" "The Wine Manager and I"; in *The Paris Review*: "Yet You Turn to the Man"; in *Quick Fiction*: "Now This"; in *Tin House*: "Colonial Revival"; in *Two Serious Ladies*: "The Locket."

"Shh" appeared in *Pets: An Anthology* (Tyrant Books, 2020), and "Master Framer" was reprinted in *We'll Never Have Paris* (Repeater Books, 2019).

ACKNOWLEDGMENTS

Thank you to these editors. I would especially like to thank Diane Williams, editor of *NOON*, for publishing my first story to appear in print and for continuing to support and challenge my work for the past ten years; this collection would not exist without her.